"We are advising all gay men in the New York area to be especially careful who they pick up these days. There is no doubt that a dangerous psychopath is on the loose, and his victims are all homosexual men who dance at the city's discos, bars, and theaters. Be especially wary if you're blond haired, are of medium height, with blue eyes, and you perform at any of the gay hangouts. The killer is believed to be very well-built, possibly a weight lifter, a loner, and he frequents gay discos and sex theaters."

—A flyer distributed
at gay night spots by NYPD,
November 24, 1980

Also by JASON FURY:

Eric's Body

The
ROPE ABOVE,
the BED BELOW

Jason Fury

Originally published by Badboy.

Copyright © 1994, 2001 by Jason Fury

978-1-5040-3000-7

Distributed in 2016 by Open Road Distribution
180 Maiden Lane
New York, NY 10038
www.openroadmedia.com

For the one and only—Big Bill Jackson

Foreword

This book is based on fact: a brief era in American gay history which will never be seen again. By the end of 1980, choices for homosexual men in New York City for unlimited sexual adventures were phenomenal. For the sociable, bars, discos, the cruisy docks, and Central Park beckoned with thousands of available partners. For the shy, anonymous sex galore was abundantly available in the darkness of gay movie houses and the dimly lit baths. But a new platform for flamboyant exhibitionism occurred literally on the stages of the new sex theaters which flourished in late 1980. And none was as shameless, notorious, and ablaze with impudent debauchery than the Show Palace near 42nd Street and which still hums along lustily today, but at a more sedate pace. The Ritz Male Follies of this novel is based loosely on this legendary sex showcase, along with the fabled little Ramrod Theater, long gone but unforgettable for its vibrant sleaziness. Anyone who ever experienced the incredible Roman Orgy Nights at the Show Palace will recognize my depictions as hardly exaggerated. This was the last outburst of feverish hedonism before the plague years began. In this book, I've tried to evoke some of the acts, the backdrops and the ambiance I knew well before it all became only a memory by the dreary mid-1980s.

Jason Fury
December 31, 1993
New York City

"I run to Death and Death meets me as fast and all my pleasures are like yesterday."

—John Donne

NOVEMBER 19, 1980—11:17 P.M.

Over the slippery sidewalks and empty streets he hurried, beneath the icy rain and past shards of frozen snow.

Killer or no killer, Alex had to get out of that rat hole of a room tonight. It had been a week since he had stripped at the Nobody Home Bar,

11

and he was down to his last buck. If he had $10, he could go to the rocking Show Palace and win that $100 they were giving away in the amateur strip contest. He would win it. One look at his golden bod, and they'd flip. But he had only a dollar, and since it was Friday night, he could zip down to Bloody Mama's where 99 cents would get you all the draft you wanted. And maybe he could find a cute trick with some jack who would give him $10—maybe $20—for a good roll in the hay.

Alex whirled around. Someone was following him. He just knew it. It was only a few blocks from the hotel to Bloody Mama's, but he could swear someone had been hurrying right behind him. There were plenty of dark doorways to hide in. The city had closed up early because of the snowstorm.

Well, fuck it all! He was used to guys following his swishy little ass, whistling, propositioning him right on the sidewalks. Maybe they'd heard he'd give head in an alleyway or in the entrance of a building for money. He didn't give a shit anymore. Since coming to the Big Apple from Georgia, he had lost the last trace of modesty.

He rubbed his cheek where that bozo had whacked him around that afternoon. The prick promised him $20 if he would allow himself to be knocked around a little. Like a fool, Alex had agreed because he was dead broke and the john really was cute: beefy and macho with a cute ass and a cock that wouldn't stay down.

But then the wacko began beating him, and he wouldn't stop even when Alex screamed. After knocking him clear across the hotel room, the bastard threw on his clothes, gave Alex the finger, and left—without paying him one fucking penny.

This time I'll be more careful. Especially with that wacko who's been going around strangling and hacking up male strippers. Two were already dead. Newspapers said there was a definite pattern. Both victims were boyish, husky, had blond hair, blue eyes.

Like me, Alex thought uneasily. A Yellow Cab splashed past, filled with people who were snug and warm, while Alex got sprayed with slush. Fuck them. Fuck Buster at Nobody Home for not letting him come back and strip. So what if he did get too wild after a few beers and tried doing guys right there at the counter.

Maybe Pete was right when he said I should stay home tonight. Pete was the desk clerk at the miserable Hotel Sun, where Alex had a tiny room. Pete was middle-aged and balding and ignored who Alex brought up to his room—in return for a blowjob every day.

Alex loved entering the warm, noisy, beery Bloody Mama. Men in leather jackets and dark glasses humped on the tiny dance floor. People whooped and laughed. Alex loved the other smells mingling with beer: Royal Bain de Champagne, Negron, Chanel perfumes, sweaty bodies, and sex. You could have fun in the dark corners if you were discreet.

Alex slapped down his one dollar and began pouring the cold beer down his throat. Oh, Jesus, this was great! These guys weren't staying home,

quaking in their beds because of the gay slasher.
Alex felt safer here than in the grungy hotel.

"Gimme some hot stuff, baby, tonight!" Donna
Summer wailed.

Alex whirled out onto the packed floor to dance
alone. He still wore his old leather jacket and red
muffler. The moist khaki paws hugged his cute
butt. Rain had plastered his curls against his
forehead, making him look much younger than
his thirty-four years. Why, I could pass for sixteen!

A plump man dressed all in leather with purple-
tinted aviator glasses rushed up to him. "You're my
Marilyn!" he slurred through his wet mustache.
"Are you really Marilyn? You look like her. Oh, you
jes' turn me on so!"

He guided Alex into a dark corner and pulled
his hand down to his crotch.

"Feel my cock, Marilyn," he panted. "Just kiss
it some, Marilyn. You're making me so hard!"

What the hell! Alex sighed, kneeling down and
covering the stranger's cock with his mouth. He
pretended it was the sadistic wacko's dick and
sucked eagerly on it because the bastard really
had been pretty damned hot. Hey, this wasn't too
bad, although it reeked of Jade East cologne. It
thickened quickly and Alex darted his tongue into
the piss-slit. The leatherman gasped, pulled
Alex's head closer and shot his wad.

Alex kept swallowing, surprised by the abundance of the man's orgasm. He wanted to stay on
it longer, but the stranger pushed him away, but-
toned up and rushed back out onto the floor.

Before Alex could stand up, another man shoved his cock into his mouth.

Wow, this man was something else, and what a dick! It was one of those beer-can-sized types, and he kept swiveling his hips, ramming it in indifferently until Alex felt his mouth pressed against a smoothly shaven pubic area.

Barely able to breathe, he began taking air in through his nostrils and thrilled to this stud's technique. His jeans had fallen down to his ankles, and Alex caressed the firm buttocks, the scrotum, and finally pushed the cock away enough so that the tip popped out for a moment.

Once again, his tongue sought the urethra and he dug it deep inside it, causing the stranger to moan in appreciation. Alex glanced up then and was stunned by the beauty of his anonymous stud.

The man's denim jacket was thrust away from his chest. Tremendous pectorals bulged out, the nipples as thick and long as pencil erasers, his stomach rippled. Suddenly the man began shooting. At first, Alex thought he was pissing when several streaks of transparent wetness hit the wall. But he realized it was only an abundance of lubricant. And then the real stuff jetted out—thick streams of sperm spattering against Alex's face.

Alex was so excited that he crammed the erection back into his mouth and expected this stallion to pull out—they usually did after the first one. To his delight, though, the satyr let him suck on it ferociously until it was hard again. Once more, Alex felt the stalk throb and then his mouth overflowed with another ejaculation.

The man pulled him to his feet and covered his mouth with his lips, kissing him deeply, guiding Alex's hands over the magnificent chest, the stomach and back to the phallus.

Alex couldn't believe it. Glancing down, he saw the cock was still fully erect and after a few jerks, more whiteness streamed out.

"Wow, oh, wow!" he whispered, looking up into the handsome face. "I can't believe this! You've just shot your third wad."

"That's nothing," the man smiled. "When it's somebody as good as you, I can do it all night."

He was nearly naked, his jeans around his boots, his jacket thrust aside and while Alex massaged his muscles the hunk said his name was Mark. He was a premed student at NYU, he had just come out of the closet, and he couldn't get enough sex.

"You look kinda like John Travolta or Warren Beatty or some movie star." Alex laughed. "Oh, man, I can't believe my luck, finding you here, Mark. It's such a shitty night."

Mark's hair was unfashionably long. The disco fad was dying and short hair was in. But it flowed so beautifully around those broad shoulders. The dark glasses gave him a mysterious air.

"Yeah, it *is* real shitty out there. Hate to go back to the dorm. You're so damned hot, I wish we had a place where we could really get it on. If you think this is good, you ought to see what I can do in bed. Feel my ass."

Alex's hands slid over Mark's hips and deep into the high mounted rump. His finger slid easily into Mark's asshole, and it began sucking on the first digit. He was perfectly smooth all over. Alex sank down to his knees again and crammed the still turgid organ into his mouth but Mark pulled it out.

"Say, let's do it right, Alex. You got a place nearby?" He began pulling up his jeans and buttoning his jacket.

"Well, uh, yeah, in a way, Mark, but you see, I vowed I wouldn't bring anybody home because of this nut-job running around slicing up strippers. You see, that's what I do."

"I thought you looked familiar. You dance at the—don't tell me—at the Nobody Home Bar."

"Wow, you have seen me then! Hey, I feel famous. But you do understand, don't you, Mark?"

The gorgeous stud nodded slowly. "Yeah, I do. I'm sorry, Alex. I felt something really hot going on between us. Maybe next time."

He turned to leave. Alex groaned, scanning that incredible ass, those shoulders, that cock bulging against the thin denim.

Grabbing Mark's strong arm, he whooped, "Fuck the killer! Come on baby. I'm just a few blocks away!"

Mark smiled, bent down, kissed him, and whispered, "Let me go first. My boyfriend is that big guy at the bar. I don't want him to see me leaving. Wait five minutes and join me."

Last dance..." Donna Summer moaned as Alex finally joined his new lover.

"You gonna kill me?" Alex mocked, as he unlocked his hotel room.

"Don't start that again!" Mark sighed and leaned down to kiss him. "Hurry up, man, let's get this show on the road. I wanna start fucking. Just feel me."

Alex rubbed the wonderful-looking bulge and groaned. "I'm 'bout ready to cream me jeans. Wait a sec—let me light the candle to make it look more cozy." Soon a golden flicker lit up the tiny chamber.

"Hey, not bad!" Mark nodded, dwarfing the cell-like room.

But Alex knew he lied. There was never enough money to beautify this roach trap, but he had made a valiant effort. On a folding table sat a hot plate, a breadbox, cans of tuna, and a big jar of Peter Pan Peanut Butter. Over the sink with the rust stain was a poster of porn star Al Parker, his famous dark erection aimed upward. On the narrow bed was a pink spread with red pillows.

The radiator pipes clanged as Alex opened the window and pulled in a gallon of cheap Chablis. He filled up two Dixie cups and gave one to Mark.

"May you come a dozen more times before you leave here," he grinned, staring down at Mark's formidable basket. Saying nothing, the visitor kicked off his boots.

"Let's get going," he said, smoothing back his long hair. "I can't wait. If you need to tinkle, then do it now. Once I get going, I don't want to stop."

He's wearing a wig, Alex thought. But then, lots of gay men did on the weekends. Still halfway in the closet, they didn't want anybody to recognize them.

"The bathroom's down the hall," Alex said. "I'm

going to run down and do pee-pee, and when I get back, you'd better have that cock ready and rarin' to go."

"Believe me, I'll be ready." Mark smiled

But when Alex returned, Mark still wore his clothes and handed him a refill of wine. "Let's have one more toast. To the future."

Alex swallowed his and grimaced. Yuck! Someday he hoped he could afford good wine that wasn't so bitter. Eagerly, he stripped naked and slid beneath the red sheets.

Mark pulled off his jacket. His muscles gleamed and rippled in the gold candlelight. Next came his jeans. *He could be a movie star,* Alex thought. Incredible muscles and that glorious ass, covered by white skivvies. But what was that black circle around his waist? A belt of some kind. Maybe it was one of those things athletes wore to keep their waist trim.

Mark still stood with his back to Alex and turned his head to stare at him over his shoulder.

"What—what'cha—cha lookin' at?" Lord, he felt so drunk all of a sudden! He could barely move his mouth. His whole body was floating.

"You look like a Christmas angel." Mark smiled. "I could see you hanging on a tree."

Alex opened his mouth to say something clever—but nothing came out. *I can't be drunk!* But it was as if Novocain flowed through his veins. That last cup of wine—what the fuck was in it? He tried sliding a leg over the edge of the bed, but he fell to the floor. Mark picked him up easily and laid him back down.

"Last"—Alex gasped, attempting to sit up —"last dance," he finished stupidly. Why did he say that? What *was* that black thing around Mark's waist? Suddenly it loosened and slid to the floor—like a snake.

Mark picked it up and held it between his hands, snapping it. Rope. A leather rope, Alex thought. Terror began to flow into his veins now.

"Wha—wha." he gasped.

"I carry this with me when I want to have fun." Mark grinned. Candlelight distorted his shadow on the wall so that he resembled a giant cobra, coiling and undulating.

Alex saw himself from a distance, moving a hand beneath his pillow and over the edge of the mattress. He kept a knife there. But just before his fingers grasped the handle, a fist smashed into his face.

The same fist knocked his teeth out as if there were corn kernels and dug down savagely into his throat until Alex conjured up a weak spasm of strength to kick and fight back.

He felt the leather rope coil around his throat. He watched the other end thrown over the old radiator pipe near the ceiling.

With a powerful tug, the maniac pulled the cord and Alex rose up into the air, right above his scarlet bed. Fury and desperation sliced through his darkness. He thrashed and clawed the air. But blood gushed down his throat, and there was no air to breathe.

"Have you ever prayed, Alex?" grinned the man who called himself Mark. "You tempted me and made me do an unholy thing. You shouldn't have done that."

"Last dance..." Alex thought. A blur of images raced through his brain...the backseat of a car in Georgia, the cock of a young boy in his mouth... men in three-piece suits stuffing dollar bills into his G-string...a river of blood foaming into the horizon.

Mark's face was radiant as he moved closer and when he held up the old-fashioned straight razor, the metal glinted in the candlelight.

Outside, the winter wind had picked up again and whipped cans and trash down the alleyway. Sleet ticked, ticked against the windows.

And there was no one below to hear the horrific growl of a man's last gasp before a razor cut into his body.

PART I

The Curtain Rises

"The death scene was so grisly that even veteran cops became sick. Two had to leave the room, they were so overcome. The victim, Alex Tart, was sexually butchered and hung from an old radiator pipe like a carcass. An expert on serial murders, Dr. Jacob Livingston of Columbia University, told me that this is only the beginning; for when a psychopath tastes blood, it whets his appetite for more."

—Bert Colman, WCBS–TV,
November 22, 1980

CHAPTER ONE

I was the hottest male stripper on the Gay White Way.

And if you were among the thousands passing along 46th Street and Broadway in late November 1980, you couldn't have missed me.

There I was, bigger than life on the huge billboard above the marquee of the Ritz Male Follies: BRETT, THE BODY BEAUTIFUL! PLUS, THE BIGGEST DISCO BOYS ON BROADWAY! I was shown wearing as little as the law would allow: short-shorts cut high up on the hip and hanging down to my cock, a leather vest, a cowboy hat and me, winking invitingly, flashing a wicked smile and two six-shooters aimed at the observer.

Surrounding me were some of the faces of the other strippers: Pepe, the Mexican cutie-pie, famed for being able to suck his own dick; Samson, the black giant from Africa, whose enormous prick was never soft; and Danny, the surfer from Australia whose routine with dildos had even the most jaded burlesque fan wide-eyed.

Hundreds of men drooled over me, and I had my pick of them all. But then, in early November, my stepbrother Steve moved in, trouble began, and everything changed.

I often wondered who our real parents were.

Both Steve and I had been adopted from the same orphanage, and although they were of completely different blood, we felt a powerful attraction for each other.

It was as if we were real brothers, but while I never grew to be more than five-foot-five, Steve kept growing and growing until he towered over me at more than six-feet-four. Even before high school, he was already working out with weights and developing a powerful torso.

And then there were all those times in bed when we had played around with each other. Although I felt faint from desire to do more than "spank the monkey," Steve was insistent that it go no further. Our stepfather had brayed and preached about the evils of perverted sex and how the devil had a fire ready to roast us if we dared give in.

Cuter than Steve Reeves and with enormous muscles, my stepbrother was confused about his sexuality. Although he wanted men, he had been taught to fight his desire as something evil. I had always had the hots for him but his repeated rejections increased the tension between us.

Worse, just a week after he moved into my fabulous little aerie in the spooky old Vanderbilt Arms on 34th Street, we were given notice by the landlord that we would have to be out by Christmas. The building was going co-op, and only the very rich could live there. That excluded me.

Even more ominous, the world of male strippers in Manhattan was suddenly under siege by a killer who hunted down some of our members and then chopped them up.

Where my world had been a wild party up until then, a shadow was growing over it, and I can remember exactly the moment I realized this.

The morning of November 22, 1980, began the way it had for the past four weeks since Steve came to live with me. Rain was freezing on the big windows of our cozy retreat, fourteen floors above Broadway. Below, traffic was a dismal blur of gray and white, with red dots of cabs gliding along.

Steve, nearly naked, still lay in bed, watching the TV news. A quilt was pushed down to his

27

hips, revealing his spectacular torso which gleamed and bulged in the wintry light. It was obvious why he had won the Mr. North Carolina and Mr. Dixie trophies for the most muscular body. His pecs were enormous, as big as the black pillows propped behind his head. His stomach was ridged with sharply cut abs, and his biceps looked like softballs. Curly black hair crowned a square face with baby-blue eyes.

Every night at the Ritz, Steve created a minor sensation when he came to pick me up. All the dancers wanted to ball with him or, at least, to see him strip naked onstage during our popular "Amateur Night," where the winner received $100.

He was still very green in many ways, though, and was still shocked by my profession. But Steve was learning fast. As I brought our tray of breakfast things to him, I thought: *If my stripper buddies could see him now, they'd get instant hardons.*

"Brett! Look, another murder! Another stripper!"

I put the tray down on the nightstand and jumped in bed with him. He hugged me close and together we watched the chilling news scene.

"We now have a live shot of the Hotel Sun," chattered the shivering reporter, standing beneath a dripping umbrella. "The police are preparing to bring out the latest victim of the serial killer. Police identify the dead man as Alex Tart, a male dancer at the Nobody Home Bar."

"Oh, my God!" I gasped. "I knew him! He was

this pathetic little guy who'd strip sometimes at
the Ritz on the weekends. Lord, he was a wild
child. No wonder"

"Shh, look!"

A man in the studio was holding up a city map
where large black circles were visible. The first
one, he said, pointing to a location on Christopher
Street, was where the first victim had been killed.

"The second victim was murdered in a cheap
hotel on 14th Street. Alex Tart, the third victim,
was found in his hotel room on 21st Street. As
you can see, the sites seem to move closer to mid-
town Manhattan."

Steve nuzzled my face. "Shit, this is getting too
weird! It looks like the psycho is coming closer in
this direction. We're moving back to North Carolina!"

"Cut it out." I smiled, pushing him back on the
pillows. "Stop worrying about me now. I can take
care of myself. And what nut is going to mess
with me while a mountain of muscles like you is
always around. Not to mention my buddies at the
theater. Especially Samson, the black giant."

But my voice stopped when we heard the
reporter conclude, "Police say each of the victims
as five-feet-five to five-feet-six inches tall, well
built and had blond hair and blue eyes."

"See!" Steve bellowed, sitting up again. "See?
That's why I'm worried about you. That's you to
a T!"

Inwardly, I was shaken out of my cocky com-
placency. As someone who stripped naked and
had sex before thousands of men each week, I had
built up a tremendous following. Each night I

received a dozen or more propositions. Love letters, complete with Polaroid shots of naked admirers, were delivered to my dressing room each day. Men had stalked me, threatened to kill me if I didn't ball with them. I managed to handle them all with a sense of humor. Only rarely had I been forced to call the cops.

Steve embraced me again, and I kissed his warm neck. "Don't make me so jittery, Steve. I make great money. And where else would I get paid to ball in public?"

He answered me as he had done a thousand times since childhood. He leaned down and kissed me—not just a stepbrotherly peck. His tongue slid down into my mouth, and my hands massaged his strong back. Then I began rubbing the huge pecs which symbolized his tremendous strength. Lowering my face, I began to suck his nipples which instantly hardened into thick, long nuggets of flesh.

From his chest, my mouth nibbled down to his flat stomach, which sank in even deeper at the touch of my lips. How deep his navel was, I thought, swirling my tongue into it. By now, his bulge was so big that it tented his white Jockey shorts.

Was this the moment I had dreamed of finally happening? We had played around like this before, but he had never let me put my mouth down there. It was sinful, he explained which was another reason why he wanted me to quit my job. Each time I let some man use his mouth on me or I did the same to him, I was sinning.

I yanked Steve's shorts down and his hard-on sprang free, standing straight up, a beer-bottle-thick phallus with a rosy round tip, still half-shrouded by a large wattle of foreskin. I pulled it down, ran my finger over and inside the gaping slit which was oozing out abundant bubbles of lubricant. Steve's breathing quickened.

He had no pubic hair. I shaved him smooth and gleaming twice a week, so now I licked his white skin. My mouth moved closer toward its goal. I could smell the spermy, macho scent of his erection. I saw it pulsing slightly in time to his heartbeat. I wrapped my fists around it, leaving several more inches at the top. My tongue began its descent into his urethra but just as it reached the opening... Steve covered everything with his big hands.

We had gone through this too many times for me to be outraged. I moved his hands away quickly and grasped his hard-on again. For some reason, he saw nothing "sinful" about my jerking him off, and so I began.

I loved to watch his big balls bulge up with each downward thrust of my fists. His slit widened even more, and I ran the tip of my thumb into it, making him gasp. A sudden burst of lubricant popped out, a certain sign that orgasm was not far away.

To watch his fantastic body writhe and tense and sparkle with sweat was a sight everyone seeking true beauty should have witnessed. His pink lips parted, is white teeth caught his lower lip, making it wet. His testicles had tightened to the point that they had nearly vanished into his scrotum.

His fists grasped the black sheets, his hips arched slightly, and then he gasped, "Okay, it's coming up!"

A stream of lubricant shot up into the air, followed by two more powerful jets. I felt his cock throb, and then he began blowing out his sperm. Like lengths of white rope, they lobbed straight up into the air, to be followed by several more spurts onto his stomach.

From the roll of Bounty paper towels we kept nearby for these daily occurrences, I cleaned him up while he just lay there, watching me. Then he sighed, "We shouldn't have done that. It ain't right."

"Oh, get off that, big guy," I laughed. "You loved it! Steve, look, you're still hard."

His glistening red organ hadn't softened at all. I began massaging it and felt it responding. "You've got more backed up in there."

"Yeah," he grunted, "it sure feels like it. Jerk it out."

Within minutes, he was ejaculating once more, even larger than the first one. Like vanilla pudding, it lay in thick puddles on his stomach. "You must've been really horny, bro." I grinned as he got to his feet.

"I dreamed I was fucking a cunt," he mumbled.

"Yeah, sure. You should discover the joy of getting sucked off."

"By you?"

"Of course, and about a dozen male strippers at the Ritz!"

He grinned, shaking his head. "You've always got sex on your mind."

"With you around, who wouldn't?"

"I gotta hurry or I'll be late for work."

He worked evenings and nights at the New York Health Spa and was one of their most popular instructors. This would do, he said, until his break came through in modeling or acting. He had to go in early today because a flu epidemic had knocked out half the spa's staff.

I had his coffee and buttered bagel waiting for him by the time he finished dressing. He wore a heavy jacket, ski cap, and boots because the weather was brutal. His pink cheeks, lips and sparkling eyes made him look like the perfect Eagle Scout.

He gulped down his food. Then we went to the door, and he kissed me for a long time. I felt his crotch and could feel its hardness. Oh, how I wanted to suck him off!

"Woo, I'd better get going before I shoot off again." He grinned. Then his face tightened: "You keep the door locked now, hear? And don't have anything to do with that nut-case down the hall. I heard him muttering and crying last night when I got off the elevator."

"You mean that cute Sam O'Brien? He's harmless, Steve. And you know something? I'd love to ball with him. You've seen his cock. He's as big as you. Umm, I can just feel it sliding up my ass!"

I loved teasing Steve because he took everything so seriously. Now his eyes widened until he saw I was teasing.

"You had me believing you there. I'm serious, now. There's something weird about that guy. And why they rented him that tower room is strange, too."

"He's one of the security guards," I explained, walking Steve to the elevator. "They want him living here in case anybody needs him. There are so many empty apartments in this building, all kinds of crazies can move in."

But after Steve left, I smiled. I was very serious about getting to know the eccentric Sam O'Brien better. He was a powerful red-haired Irishman who never wore a stitch of clothing and left his door open for us to see everything God had given him. And God had been generous to him. No one else lived on our tiny floor, which was at the top of the building. So a shiver of sexual excitement went through me as I thought of being alone with this particular security guard.

Since Steve knew zilch about keeping up an apartment, I spent the morning buying groceries at the corner Sloan's and picking up our laundry across the street from the Korean cleaners.

Waiting for the light to change, I stood on the corner of Broadway and studied our apartment building. It already resembled a huge mausoleum. Only Steve and I and a few others were left. Our old bastard landlord, Jake Strouff, wanted us out before Christmas. We'd have to start looking for another place any day now.

I nodded to the two Latino guards in the lobby who studied me with keen interest, rubbing themselves suggestively. It wasn't everyday they got a close-up look at the "King of Burlesque," as Arthur Bell had described me in his column for the *Village Voice*.

Then I got off the elevator. The corridor was dark and cold. Only one light cast its illumination. I put down my bags to unlock the door quickly. Suddenly a strong arm wrapped around my throat.

"Your time has come, you fucking little slut!"

Twirling around, I looked up into the laughing face of Sam O'Brien. Except for a towel, he was naked. I smacked his big chest, which made him laugh even more. His green eyes danced with glee.

"You bastard, Sam O'Brien! I nearly gave you a karate chop that would have left you singing soprano!"

"Did I really scare my favorite stripper? Hey, you're shaking!"

"It's just the cold." And lust, I thought, because he was one of these big, powerful men who managed to look more naked with just a towel on than without one. His skin was white, smooth, and bulging with enough muscles to indicate that he worked out with weights. And when he put an arm around my shoulder and guided me toward his room, I thought, Good God, he's so hot!

"Come to my room, my golden-haired slut, for a cup of fresh Colombian coffee I just made."

"No. My stepbrother thinks you're the butcher who's killing off the gay strippers."

"Yeah, I know." Sam grinned, completely

unperturbed. "I like shocking him. But you know, for a guy who looks so fantastic, he sure does act like Mary Poppins. Enter my room, my sweet, so I can rape you."

"Ha, no chance of that, Sammy boy."

He had made his studio cozy and warm. A vivid patchwork quilt of reds and blues and yellows covered the captain's bed. On the wall were pictures of him bulging his muscles in a physique competition—and there was one of him wearing the high collar and attire of a priest."

"Sam, you really were a priest, weren't you? I thought you were joking."

He brought me a mug of steaming coffee and sat down on the edge of his desk. "That's me, all right. I just couldn't keep my hands off those beautiful, big-dicked Italian boys. And when I finally sucked one off while his cousin fucked me, I knew exactly where my head lay. So I've been a slut for the past year."

He said he came to New York and was trying to make up for lost time. He loved getting gang-banged in the balcony of the Adonis Theater, sucking countless cocks in the baths, and getting his sucked off relentlessly in the Ramble area of Central Park.

"I'd sure like to blow your stepbrother," Sam said. "He packs a bulging basket. And that ass! Wow, I saw him in his jogging shorts last week when it wasn't raining, and I wanted to get on my knees and suck him off right there."

"Everybody wants to blow Steve, including me, but no such luck."

"I could see him in a hot porno film, getting

36

fucked by Johnny Holmes or Jack Wrangler. Umm, I'm getting hard just thinking about it."

His thin towel was certainly rising, like a pole beneath a tent. He undid the towel, which fell to the floor.

"What'd ya think about this?" he grinned, grasping his erection and flapping it at me. He had a bull dick, dark, ugly, rough but delicious looking. Like Steve, his foreskin half-hid the tip so now he ripped it back, letting the big pink meatball pop out.

"See? I keep myself shaved. Look at my butt-hole, Brett. Ain't it a beauty?"

He bent over his desk and spread his round white ass. It really was a glorious sight. He made his pink rectum wink at me while he ground his stormy length of meat against the hard edge of the desk. Back and forth he rubbed it until it was halfway down to his knee.

I couldn't resist him. He had one of these beautifully white bodies without a blemish. I fell to my knees and buried my face in his ass, wriggling my tongue up into his pliant hole. At the same time, I grabbed his cock and began milking him. The harder I squeezed, the better he liked it.

"Wow, oh, wow!" he panted. "That's dynamite. Been wanting to ball with you ever since I came up here. I see you at the theater and—stay down there, honey, I wanna mouth-fuck you."

He braced my head against the desk, stooping slightly to push the tip of his hard-on into my mouth. I hugged his hips to bring them closer until finally he had filled up my ·throat. It was a fantastic cock to suck on. He didn't want it gentle and sweet. I squeezed and mashed his testicles, running my fingers up into his butt while almost gagging on his meat. Finally it pulsated, and my throat was drenched with semen. Lord, it felt like a pint being pumped out. But he didn't take it out. I knew he wanted me to keep on sucking.

While doing so, he reached down for a cloth bag beside the desk. From the corner of my eye, I saw him remove and open a black box. Inside was an amazing array of dildos. He chose one that looked like a baby's arm. Then he removed a length of black leather from the bag.

I drew back, unsure what he was going to do, suddenly fearful but I relaxed as I saw him wrap the leather tightly around his genitals so that his cock became even darker and hard. He expertly inserted the enormous tip of the dildo up into his butt and gradually sat down on it.

Then he beckoned me to resume my sucking while he began to rise and fall slightly on his artificial cock. His erection was really a sight to see now. While sucking on his dickhead, my fists were milking him brutally. He was joyous.

His beautiful white torso rippled, gleamed with sweat and my tongue dug deep into his slit. Suddenly, I felt a definite pulsation and, once more, a torrent of lubricant and semen jetted down my throat.

Still panting, he turned around and motioned me to continue fucking him with the dildo. He ground his still-thick cock against the rough edge of the desk, mashing it without mercy until it was stiff again. When he ejaculated again, I watched his butthole clamp hungrily around the dildo like a mouth.

When he turned around, his face was still flushed. He bent down to take my cock in his mouth. I smiled. "Sorry, but I've got to save mine for the theater tonight. Will you be there?"

"Wow, you'd better believe it! After this work-out, I'm sure I'll be raring to go again."

He put his arms around me and kissed me. I felt his sticky cock begin to stiffen again.

"Sam, I've got to go!" I gasped, pulling away and watching him begin go slap his penis across his palm like a rubber mallet. "You're amazing! You're like my stepbrother—you can come again and again. Not many guys can do that."

"That's why I'm getting your brother's cherry somehow." He grinned. He was still jerking his meat when I picked up my bags in the hallway and hurried into my apartment. It would soon be time for me to appear as Brett, the Body Beautiful. I was looking forward to turning on all those hundreds of men and of actually having sex onstage with at least one of them. I wanted everyone to see what a sexual athlete Sam O'Brien was.

Chapter Two

Although the weather was brutal, I still enjoyed my walk along Broadway toward the Ritz.

Just within a few blocks of each other was probably the largest concentration of gay hangouts in the world. And I knew them well.

I was never a bar person, so I never frequented

them. But when I first came to Manhattan two years before, I loved going to the David Cinema, at 236 East 54th Street and living in the orgy room, where men were packed over the weekends. You could suck cock until your jaws were sore or lean against the wall and let men do you until you could come no more. Now Jack Wrangler was appearing in *New York Construction Co.*

Just a block away was the swanky little 55th Street Playhouse, where *Joe Gage's Closed Set* was packing them in. Behind the screen was a wonderful make-out area. I couldn't count the orgasms I'd enjoyed back there, especially the night Al Parker appeared for the gala opening of his new triple-X-rated classic, *Inches*. Men were doing each other in the auditorium and especially back behind the screen.

The Broadway Baths was at 218 West 49th Street. For the price of a towel, you could enjoy wall-to-wall sex. It was a favorite spot for many of the dancers and Ritz fans to go after the show and let off steam. A favorite room was the "sling" chamber, where men would put their legs and arms into the slings and let themselves be fisted.

The Big Top Cinema was at 1604 Broadway at 49th Street, and *In Search of the Perfect Male* was enjoying record business. Never mind that the gay flicks rotated from theater to theater and you could still find the same titles playing a year later. To most of the patrons, watching the movies was of secondary interest. They wanted some hot action.

I paused to study the marquee of the swinging,

wild little Ramrod Theater, also on 49th Street, which was still advertising Marathon Disco Fever and featuring in person Keith Anthoni in his notorious one-man show, "You Will Not Believe Your Eyes." It wasn't every day that you saw someone sucking his own cock onstage. *Christmas Time* was the main movie being shown with Big, Big Sly, plus Joey, Mike, and acts of passion. That last was a code word to the savvy that you would also see live sex onstage.

The Night Shift at 777 Eighth Avenue at 47th Street offered nearly everything a sensualist needed for erotic release: "glory holes...slings... lounges... bunkrooms and our new mirror oom."

Between 45th and 46th was the shadowy Eros Cinema, which was not only having the premiere of the movie, *Grease Monkey,* but was featuring "live onstage" the film's lusty young stars: Lee Marlin, Nick Rogers, and the very popular Kip Noll.

I still loved dropping in occasionally at the Gaiety Burlesque at 201 West 46th Street, just around the block from the Ritz. That night it was advertising DYNAMIC MARATHON WITH 12 BOYS! and was showing that ever-popular *Boys of Venice* and *The Destroying Angel.*

Just down the street on Eighth Avenue was the world-famous Adonis Theater, immortalized in the movie, *A Night at the Adonis.* That night, it was showing a Kip Noll double-treat, *Westside Boys* and again, *Boys of Venice.* Around the block, the best blowjobs in town could be found at the dismal little hole-in-the-wall King Cinema, which was showing *The Portrait of Dorian Gay*. In winter, there was no heat, and I could imagine the bleak scene inside the theater. But for some strange reason, it attracted a loyal clientele. Usually the men sitting in the back rows were ferocious cocksuckers. You just stood behind them, dropped your drawers, and they would take over. One of my favorites was a slender, bald man who always wore a ski cap.

He had a fantastic technique of tonguing the slit and taking all the cock down to the pubic bone, regardless of its length. One night I watched him taking on two men at one time, going from one hard-on to the other, passionately sucking and wanting more after the guys came.

And probably the Ritz's biggest competitor was the wild and woolly Show Palace at 670 Eighth Avenue, near 42nd Street. Their ads screamed: PINBALL! CRUISING! MORE! KINKY! BIZARRE! They, too, offered an Amateur Night competition with the winner winning $100. That was how I got my start a year before, and I was on my way. The Palace was also featuring a "turkey gobble" onstage and veterans quickly picked up on its meaning: the strippers would be sucked on stage.

I glanced at the other "legit" theaters as I hurried along. *9 to 5* had just opened with Jane Fonda and Dolly Parton, and the very hunky William Hurt was starring in the sci-fi movie, *Altered States*. An Australian movie had just opened to good reviews, too: *Breaker Morant* which I heard featured some handsome, beefy boys from Down Under.

Maybe someday I'd have a chance to see some of these movies, but I was too obsessed with my world at the Ritz, which gave me everything I wanted. Within that beautiful old theater which Matt Dempsey had renovated with red carpets, cushioned seats, crimson and gold lamé curtains, and a sound system second to none, I had everything I wanted.

Fame, money, and sex with the most handsome men in the world.

"Hey, look who's here! Brett, the Body Beautiful!"

"Hi, you sluts! Hey, get that hard-on out of the way. You know how easily I shock."

"They're horny out there tonight, Brett! Looka that kid on the front row! He's buck naked, and he's been jerking his meat for the past hour! Ain't it shocking?"

"Just another night at the Ritz," I drawled. Our backstage banter at the Ritz before a show was raucous, brutal, and fun. Especially on Friday nights when we made our "nut"—that big block of money which more than paid the bills and gave us our fancy salaries.

It was scuzzy and cramped behind the stage as dancers wandered around, smoking, sipping mineral water and Cokes, and snacking on M&M's, chips, and oranges. Matt Dempsey, our handsome millionaire theater owner, had fixed me up a dressing room the size of a broom closet. I loved it, though. It demonstrated that I was at the top of our very transitory profession. I realized only too well that today's Kings of Burlesque could be tomorrow's weekend strippers—those handsome guys who take their clothes off only on the weekends to make some easy money.

I began putting on my Ivy League outfit: sweater, slacks, boots, which would all hit the floor in front of nearly eight hundred men. Armand, the golden-bodied Frenchman, flopped down in the chair next to my table. He wore just a white G-string. His lean muscles danced as he grabbed a handful of jelly beans from my candy bowl.

"Where's that gorgeous stepbrother of yours?" he cooed.

"Don't worry, slut, he'll be here at midnight sharp. He doesn't want to see his stepbrother doing such evil things like getting blown or sucking cock."

Teddy, another handsome dancer, wearing only a black bikini stuck his curly head in the doorway. "Your stepbrother needs to get his dick deepthroated and that beautiful butt rimmed."

"What do you guys think I've been trying to do for a month? He only lets me jerk him off."

"You beat his meat?" squealed Pepe, the Mexican cutie who wore nothing. "*Mamma mia,* tell us about it."

And so while Al Parker was fucking some lucky stiff on the movie screen behind us, I shamelessly filled them on every facet of Steve's orgasm, including the way his muscles rippled during eruption.

Pepe, who had just finished sucking his own cock to the delight of his fans out front, was pulling on his meat again. Teddy, who had no inhibitions either, fell to his knees and began blowing the dark-skinned Pepe, who leaned against the door frame. Some of the other dancers paused to study this familiar scene.

"Pepe," I joked, "how many times have you come today? Look at Teddy's face! It's all purple! He must have your cock in his throat."

Pepe rolled his eyes comically and nodded his head, causing us all to burst out laughing. He tapped Teddy's head and the sucker pulled back, just in time to watch Pepe unload. I grabbed a paper towel just in time as he spurted a thick puddle of semen into it.

Teddy remained on his knees, panting, his face flushed and looked around. "Come on, let me suck some more, you guys! Whatsa matter with you all?"

"We've got to save it for the fans, stoopid!" I explained. "Go into the john. I'll bet Mr. Dickhead is in there."

"Say, you're right!" Teddy grinned, getting to his feet. "I blew him for an hour this afternoon, but I hate kneeling down on that sticky floor."

We all knew who Mr. Dickhead was. He was a regular who never missed a Saturday. He was a young guy, probably a college kid, who installed himself in one of the johns, stripped naked, and offered his sturdy cock to all who wanted it. I had blown him once out of curiosity and found him delicious. But, like Teddy, I hated having to kneel on that piss- and come-sticky floor.

Matt Dempsey stuck his handsome head in my

47

doorway, glanced at Teddy, who was tugging at his erection, and frowned. "Teddy, damn it all, how many times have I told you to have your sex onstage? Anyway, all of you are invited to an orgy at the Plaza Hotel after the show. Some rich Texas big-wig is putting on the dog for you sluts."

The others whooped, but I shook my head. "Sorry, but Steve's coming by and—I know, I know, I should bring him along but he's still a real innocent and he's lonely, too. No, we're going home, get in bed and—"

"So when's your stepbrother going to strip butt-naked on my stage? I'll give him $500. And if he loses his virginity to one of you guys with everybody watching, I'll add another $500."

The others gasped—not just at the money, but at the idea of Steve actually getting fucked onstage.

"Say, now you're talking, Matt. He'll decide that. I'm not forcing Steve into anything. Uh-oh, it's my number they're playing. Teddy, don't brush your cock against my pants. Your cock's drooling all over the place!"

Ruth Brown was wailing the old classic, "Daddy, Daddy," my theme song, and I listened as Eddie, our midget deejay with the velvety voice announced me.

"And now, we are proud to bring you our star attraction, the body beautiful you've all been waiting to see, not to mention his big dick and beautiful ass! the Ritz Male Follies now brings you—Brett, the Body Beautiful!"

The theater erupted into screams and applause

and whistles. My faithful fans were certainly out
there, including a healthy sprinkling of tourists
who had heard about the wild goings-on at the
Ritz. They would now have plenty to report back
to their buddies in Boise, Montgomery, and other
Bible Belt cities.

The other dancers always wanted the latest
disco hit to perform by, but I much preferred
those sexy old rhythm-and-blues classics and anything by the great Ruth Brown. I swiveled out
into the gold spotlight, my blond curls gleaming,
and gradually stripped off everything but a blue
silk bikini.

The naked kid in the front row was jerking his
cock, grinning at me, glancing down at his hard-
on with an inviting look. Suck me, suck me, he
seemed to pant. I recognized old Petey, the little
gay man and his boyfriend, a tall, dour German.
They were always sending me small gifts of
cologne, scented soap, sweaters.

The body I worked so hard to keep in top condi-
tion was now completely nude. I watched a ripple
of excitement pass over the audience. It was now
time for me to find some lucky partner and actually do it!

My eyes had become used to the darkness now,
and as I fell to my stomach and wriggled out onto
the runway which went into the audience, I saw
the face I was looking for.

Sam O'Brien sat right next to the runway, completely naked, stroking his hard-on, and now he
winked and grinned at me. Sometimes I struck
out with my random selection of "partners." The

49

guys who looked so hot performed poorly onstage, overcome with temerity and nerves. Occasionally I would strike solid gold with some lusty, uninhibited sexualist.

Faces were so close to me as I continued crawling and wriggling along the wooden walkway that I felt mouths kissing my ass, stroking it, hoarse words: "I love you! God, you're beautiful!"

When I finally reached Sam, who was causing some excitement among his neighbors because of his smashing good looks, I draped my legs over the edge of the runaway. Without hesitation, he pulled my thighs around his neck and crammed my cock into his mouth.

There was more heavy breathing from all those who watched him suck. Eddie had trained the spotlight on us so that everyone could see. Now and then, Sam would pop my cock out of his mouth and let everyone see how thick and big it was. I wasn't just feigning my sexual writhing. Sam was incredible.

I felt my come boiling for eruption and tapped Sam's bouncing head. Reluctantly, he took my hard-on out just in time. Three long streaks of whiteness jetted out among the audience, which cheered and whistled.

But Sam wasn't finished. He joined me on the runway and lay over me, thrusting my thighs around his back. His hard-on was a sight to behold—purple and furious. Without any lubrication, he began to inch it up into me.

The dancers were cheering Sam on, and I spotted many men in the audience either jerking themselves off or bending over the lap of a neighbor. Sam's body was gorgeous, too, as he continued to fuck me. It wasn't every day that we dancers found someone as handsome, big, and uninhibited as Sam.

Suddenly, he pulled out and aimed his dark erection at the audience. The lucky ones were dappled with thick gobbets of sperm.

We kissed and he laughed softly, "That was as great as I knew it would be." He shook his cock and sat back in his seat, still nude, still playing with his cock. I watched a young man in the adjoining seat bend down and take it in his mouth as I dashed behind the stage.

The other dancers praised me for my "performance," and they all swore they wanted to use Sam in their sex routines. I showered quickly and threw on a robe. I didn't want to miss a second of the act following mine.

Although I was the star of the Ritz, Matt Dempsey liked hiring a "guest star" for the busy weekends. He had to pay plenty to get the notorious but very popular Bruno from the Show Palace. Bruno's act was so wild that everyone—including me—had gone to see him. Now I wanted to see whether he had toned his act down for the classier Ritz.

"Good Times" by Chic pulsed through the theater. A red spotlight hit Bruno dressed in his favorite costume: a black biker's cap with skull and bones, black leather jacket, and pants, and boots. Besides my stepbrother and Sam O'Brien, he had one of the sexiest bodies I had ever seen.

A dark stubble gave his boyish face a rough edge, along with the sunglasses. He threw off his jacket. Powerful pecs gleamed from sweat. Each nipple was pierced, glittering with metal rings. Without even attempting to dance, he just strolled around the stage as though he were in the privacy of his bedroom.

Making no pretext at dancing, he peeled off his leather pants quickly. A gasp went up. His cock was huge and as dark and mean looking as Sam O'Brien's. Glinting in the long snout of his foreskin was another metal ring.

From his hips, he bent down and took the ring between his teeth and kept it there as he straightened up, stretching his fleshy overhang to an incredible length.

He removed the pin and ripped his skin down so the rosy tip popped out like a small tomato.

Walking down the walkway, clad just in his boots and cap, his beautiful butt swung to and fro and he kept digging fingers into his foreskin, spreading it out like dough. He was looking for a partner. From around his waist, he removed a long length of black leather which he swirled over his head like a cowboy's lasso. His eyes searched the gaping fans and settled on Sam O'Brien. One man was bending over Sam's shoulders, pulling at the thick nipples. Sam's cock was still being worked on by his neighbor.

The leather rope fell over Sam's head. A cheer went up. Sam pushed his sucker aside and bounded onto the runway. Obviously, Bruno had liked the way Sam partnered me. Judging from the

Irishman's turgid, dark hard-on, he was ready to go again.

Bruno fell to his knees and crammed Sam's hard-on into his mouth. His ability to deep-throat was legendary and we watched him relax his throat as he swallowed the dark, hard organ slowly.

Sam, standing there with his legs apart, shivered as we watched the rest of his dick vanish into the wet mouth until—finally—Bruno's mouth was pressed against Sam's shaven pubis.

We could hear Bruno's wet, strangled gulps. His head trembled as his throat went to work on Sam's hard-on. Sweat began popping out on Sam's beautiful white body. His fingers plucked at Bruno's dark curls until, finally, he tapped him on the head.

Reluctantly, Bruno released the glistening thick tube. Sam gasped as his fists milked out a huge orgasm which covered Bruno's face.

Frantically, the dancer fell on his back and raised his thighs back, pointing toward his asshole. I didn't think even Sam had enough energy to do it, but my neighbor grinned and fell on top of Bruno.

We all watched him work his still-oozing dick up into Bruno's ass. For several minutes, we watched Sam's shapely butt rise up and down as he dug deeper into Bruno. Then, once more, he pulled out to spatter the floor with his male elixir.

But Bruno was only getting warmed up. Two of the dancers brought out a low dais, covered with leather. Taking Sam's hand, Bruno went up to the sturdy table and lay down on his back. Another dancer, Calvin a butch marine type, came out completely naked. In one hand he had a big can of Crisco.

He began packing the greasy stuff over Bruno's butthole and casually popped four fingers into the cavity. Then, expertly, he slid his hand, then his wrist up into Bruno's hungry ass. Sam slathered more Crisco over Calvin's arm, all the way to the shoulder. We were spellbound to see Calvin's entire arm vanish up into Bruno's butt.

The swarthy dancer was joyous, grinning and grunting his pleasure. Calvin pulled his arm out and then clasped Sam's hand in his. Together the two fists vanished up into Bruno again, then their arms.

It was like watching an enormous dildo swivel back and forth as Bruno's butthole was stretched to an incredible degree. This ritual seemed to turn on both the fist-fuckers. Calvin's cock was standing straight up while lubricant was dripping from Sam's ever-ready phallus.

Finally the two men withdrew their fists. Towels were handed to them to clean their arms while Bruno wiped his ass.

He went to the edge of the stage and announced: "Anybody who wants to fuck me, come on up! I won't turn away anybody who's healthy and clean and wants to come! Come on, you studs! Let me do some sucking while you do the fucking!"

The naked kid on the front row jumped up on the stage, and other men, completely naked, hurried down. Soon Bruno was flat on his back again, sucking a cock and getting fucked again.

Calvin propped Sam against the wall and fell to his knees, cramming the Irishman's cock into his mouth. As Alicia Bridges sang out, "I Love the Nightlife," the other dancers, all bareass and horny, came onto the stage and their fans fought to fall down on their knees and pay them oral homage.

I caught Sam's eye. His body trembled from Calvin's energetic blowjob. He winked and whistled, as if saying: this is heaven.

Oh, how I wanted to get out there and orgy, too. But it was midnight, and Steve was waiting for me.

His eyes were wide as he beheld the sight onstage and out in the audience. Some of the dancers were worn out, though, and wanted to watch the action. They fluttered around Steve, who blushed and grinned.

"Wouldn't you like to come and join the fun?" cooed Johnny the Cowboy as he rubbed his hand over Steve's crotch. Just as he began unbuttoning my brother's jeans, Steve moved back.

"It looks like everybody's having fun," he smiled. Turning to me, he said quickly, "You ready to go?"

We were passing Bruno's dressing room, where we noticed a crowd watching something within. Steve and I were just in time to watch Sam O'Brien slide his flushed-looking cock up into Bruno's asshole.

"Push it in deeper, Sam!" Bruno squealed. "I like it rough!"

Sam had taken Bruno's leather lasso and draped it over his neck. He pulled on it as he began to fuck. Bruno's face turned red as he gasped for breath.

"Not too hard, Irishman! I want to be alive when you fuck me!"

As Steve and I left, we heard Sam slapping his partner's butt with loud, stinging blows.

And I looked down to see my stepbrother bulging out in his jeans. He had been turned on by all the wild, raucous activity. It was just another Friday night at the Ritz Male Follies.

The rain had turned to sleet as Steve and I hurried home. Neither of us liked the subway, and it was only a half-hour walk.

Rarely are the sidewalks of Manhattan deserted, but tonight only the hardy were out and about. Beneath the umbrella, we moved swiftly toward 32nd Street. Suddenly I paused.

"What's the matter?" Steve asked.

"I've got this weird feeling somebody's following us."

He looked around. Huge buildings loomed up like tombstones. Only a few shadowy figures still loitered in the doorways.

"There's nobody," Steve observed.

"Steve, I tell you I'm sure somebody was not far behind us. Let's get on home!"

He put his arm around my shoulder, and I was glad he was with me. I had fought off several muggers and too-fervent admirers which always caught them by surprise since I'm only five-foot-five. But one of the first things I did when arriving in Manhattan was to take a course in self-defense, and it had paid off on several occasions.

Inside the apartment, we both stripped naked and got into the shower. Steve's cock was jutting out so much that I couldn't move without brushing against it.

"You're horny tonight, big guy." I smiled.

He was soaping up his huge pecs and grinned. "Hell, I did come into the Ritz a little early tonight. I saw that crazy Irishman down the hall fucking you and then I saw that Bruno get fisted. Whew! That was something weird!"

I was startled by his words. Steve usually refused to discuss my job and pretended he didn't know what happened. I ran my hand along his cock, and he winced.

"Oh, man! I'm 'bout ready to blow."

"Hurry up, stud, and let's get in bed."

Again, he always wanted to play games with me when he knew I wanted to ball with him and made me spend frustrating minutes enticing him to be jerked off. But now he was actually offering it to me! What was happening to my sexually repressed stepbrother?

In bed, he continued to surprise me by grabbing me and kissing me. My hands explored his body, vanishing into the deep cleft of his ass, tickling his rectum which made him groan.

Finally he turned over on his back and nodded his head. "I'm ready, honey. Go to it."

I couldn't believe what I was hearing. Getting him to even lie there and have his meat beaten was always an obstacle course. I didn't waste any time, though. I sucked his nipples and then buried my tongue into his deep navel. Slowly, I moved to the ultimate prize whose tip brushed my cheek, streaking it with the thick lubricant oozing out.

I grasped his cock with both hands; but just as my mouth was ready to devour his bulging ball of pink meat, he covered it with his fists.

"No, no, not the mouth, baby. Just the hands."

I wanted to scream my frustration, but quickly decided that having his cock in my hands was better than not having it at all. Only a few sturdy strokes were necessary for that first load of the night to rocket up into the air, surging in thick abundance.

"Gee, you were ready to brim over, Steve." I smiled. "What you saw must have really sexed you up."

"Maybe," he sighed. "Beat it some more. I've got more backed up. Um, it's hurting really bad."

He lay there, trembling from my hand motions. I watched his slit part even more until I could see the transparent honey surging up.

My hands were slimy with his lubricant dripping over my fingers. Then he grunted, grasped the sheets, and blew out another gusher. He came two more times that night. I realized that he would make someone a wonderful lover—that prized male who was capable of multiple orgasms.

Before we turned out the light, I glanced at the wads of paper towels soaking with sperm, piled up in our trash can. "Aren't you ashamed of yourself, wasting all that paper?" I joked.

"Yeah, there's probably a pint of come in there," he grinned.

I told him about Matt Dempsey's offer—$500 to strip on Amateur Night and another $500 to let someone take his cherry publicly.

"You're kidding!" he hooted. "I've never heard of such a thing. Me, getting fucked onstage! Shi-yat!"

"This is a wild time for gay guys," I said, nestling in his arms and playing with his nipples. "Even two years ago, this would have been unthinkable. Rut they have live straight-sex shows on 42nd Street, so now they've got them for gays, too. You'd be a sensation. I'm not encouraging you to do it, but there wouldn't be any danger."

His face hardened as he turned the lamp. "You know why I'm like this. Don't you ever think of those days at home, with Stepdaddy and...I'll think about it, though. Wow, $500 just to take off my clothes and $500 more to get fucked. This is wild!"

He fell asleep quickly, but after an hour, I got up to make some hot chocolate. Something bothered me, making me uneasy. I studied my beautiful stepbrother, lying there curled up like a little boy but with the body of Hercules. He had gone through a childhood that should have sent him into a mental institution, all because of our stepfather.

I pulled back the curtains. A man stood across the street, in front of the closed Korean laundry.

He wore dark glasses and had dark hair curling around his shoulders. He was a big man, too, and he was staring straight up at me. Seeing me, he pulled up the collar of his jacket, and slinked off into the dreary night.

I checked the lock on our door and made sure the chain lock was also in place. Then I took a butcher knife from the kitchen drawer and put it beneath my mattress. I was certain that the stranger was none other than the gay killer.

PART II
Intermission

"We are advising all gay men in the New York area to be especially careful who they pick up these days. There is no doubt that a dangerous psychopath is on the loose, and his victims are all homosexual men who dance at the city's discos, bars, and theaters. Be especially wary if you're blond haired, are of medium height, with blue eyes, and you perform at any of the gay hangouts. The killer is believed to be very well-built, possibly a weight lifter, a loner, and he frequents gay discos and sex theaters."

—A flyer distributed at gay night spots by NYPD, November 24, 1980

CHAPTER THREE

Nobody but I knew of the horrors Steve had undergone as a boy growing up in a religious home in North Carolina during the 1950s and 1960s.

He was always my handsome big stepbrother; but when he was at home, he was slender and pale faced. There was a reason for that: our evangelistic stepfather, who preached at a small fundamentalist church in Carson City

He was a handsome-as-hell born-again Christian who had suddenly discovered God when he was serving two years in prison for trying to murder his own father. There, as he liked to tell everyone, God visited him and told him he would be saved if he spread the good word.

And so after marrying the meek, mousy Florence Maybrick, he settled in Carson City, adopted two sons, and proved to us that he should never have been released from prison.

Steve always seemed to have an army of private demons haunting him. Just who were his real father and mother? Were they, too, heavy brooders, depressed? Steve's dark spells didn't last long, but they seemed to come out of nowhere.

I knew that whoever my real parents were, they must have had sunny dispositions. I rarely got blue, was even-tempered and would rather laugh at trouble than give in to it.

"I wish to God I'd had your parents, too," Steve had often told me. "Nothing seems to get you down. I was born to brood."

And I would then throw my arms around the handsome boy, kiss him, and caress his big muscles. "Steve, you look so fucking fantastic, you should be thrilled! Look at me—I'm just a little runt. You look like Superman and Hercules rolled into one."

"Let's try to find out who our real parents were," Steve suggested often. Although intrigued, I resisted.

"I don't want to know," I said bluntly. "They had reason to want to give us up. What we've got now ain't all that great, but maybe our real ones were even worse."

Stepdaddy was a big, beefy man with a florid face from the secret cache of rotgut whiskey he kept. His violent, tormented soul drove him to beat us mercilessly from the time we were ten. Steve and I grew to dread the sound of our bedroom door opening, and the lock quietly latching behind him. Our stepmother pretended not to notice anything—she was a bland, cipher of a woman who believed it was a woman's duty not to interfere with what her husband did in private.

A freak accident killed my father. On a cold morning, he struck a match to light the old oil stove in the living room. Somehow, oil had seeped steadily into the stove over night. It blew up, killing him instantly.

No one but my mother shed any tears for him. My brother's face was cold and pale. By this time, he was a star athlete in high school and after graduation, he joined the marines. I began to hear rumors that Steve was letting some of his old football and basketball buddies jerk him off for money, but he wouldn't let anyone blow him. His religious conversion at age sixteen had forced him to draw the line somewhere.

But not before a last night with me. Steve had always enjoyed kissing me, even after his religious experience a few years earlier. We pooled our money together for a six-pack of beer. God wouldn't mind this minor lapse, he explained.

Our bedroom was covered with my movie idols: Elizabeth Taylor, Bette Davis, Joan Crawford. His side was plastered with bodybuilders: Steve Reeves and a young emerging superstar, Arnold Schwarzenegger.

Through that night, we sipped our beer which I really could stand, and I played with Steve's cock, jerking out a number of thick orgasms.

"Steve, tell me something," I said at dawn. "You're going your way, I'll be going mine soon. Did you like getting sucked off by those guys? I'd watch you sometimes and it seemed like you loved it—and getting fucked, too."

He closed his eyes and sighed. "If I did or didn't, it's in the past. What we did was evil! Perverted!"

"But you know watching you suck off quite a few of the farm hands! I've been thinking about it, too, and I love it."

"With you it's different. You want that to happen. The Devil made me do it. He made me do it! Good night, baby brother."

Right after he left, I graduated high school and hitchhiked to New York City.

Instantly, I felt at home. I created a sensation my first week there by tearing off my clothes at the Nobody Home Bar, getting up on the counter, and dancing.

The men loved me for my beauty. My hair was a mass of gold curls and my body was a golden bronze from sunbathing nude on the roof of the YMCA where I was staying on 34th Street.

I was offered at job as one of the go-go boys and

66

from there I danced at the Eros, then the Gaiety. By then, I had developed a strong following. Whenever I appeared onstage, my fans screamed and whistled their delight.

And when the Show Palace hired me for a week, I brought the house down, so they put my name up in lights. I was thrilled to strip naked, then go out into the audience and let my fans suck my nipples, my cock, and fuck me.

If Stepdaddy could see me now, I laughed. My ass drove the customers crazy and on orgy nights, there would be a dozen or more, waiting their turns to fuck me. I let only one or two do it; unlike my stepbrother, I was no sex machine.

One night, I teased a handsome older man in the audience who had stripped off all his clothes. Naked as a jaybird, I stooped down between his legs and sucked him off. Then he had me to climb into his lap, and he slid his hard-on in to the hilt. While fucking me, he bent down and took my erection in his mouth and made me come twice.

"You're fantastic!" he gasped after licking up my sperm from his hand. "You've got to come and perform at my new place. The Ritz Male Follies, a block away! You'll be my star performer! If you can do there what you do here, it'll be a gold mine. Oh, let me suck you again, golden boy!"

And so that was how I came to the Ritz Male Follies. From the first night, Matt Dempsey, the owner, did turn-away business. I was ballyhooed as "The Golden Boy of Burlesque," "The King of Burlesque," and "Broadway's Most Naked Star."

But I had to lay down some ground rules with

Matt and the other dancers. I wanted to save my sexual energy for the fans. They wanted to make physical contact with me, and I wanted a strictly business relationship. But Matt and I did agree to getting together at least once a week for some hot sessions. In a way, I found him to be the father figure I never had.

His mouth was tender but hungry, easily causing me to get hard. When he slid his hard-on up my ass, he did it lovingly.

Through Matt, I was able to move into a fabulous little studio at the very top of the Vanderbilt Arms, in one of the two tower chambers. My older lover also saw to it that my rent was criminally low—$200 a month. I suspected Matt was paying the difference.

My nights were wild but never dangerous. Even in those days, I was instinctively careful about sex. I never allowed anyone to come inside me. I douched each day, sometimes several times. I always carried a small bottle of Listerine and, after sucking cock, I would gargle.

I didn't want to get any of the infections I saw other dancers get. Some were so high on dope or booze that they didn't know what was happening. I drank and took nothing—except for a few drinks after my performance. I kept my body in top shape and took handfuls of vitamins because, in my profession, burnout was a given.

Suddenly one afternoon, I answered my doorbell to find Steve on my doorstep. I couldn't believe it! He looked fabulous, as powerful and muscular as any of the muscle gods of the screen.

He had won all kinds of trophies in the marines and briefly as a high-school coach in North Carolina.

But he wanted to give modeling and acting a try. We had corresponded through the years, and I had told him bluntly in my letters what I did for a living. But after we hugged for a while, and praised each other's appearance, I had him to sit down for coffee.

"I don't know whether or not you've changed your ideas about sex over the years, Steve, but I'm not apologizing for what I do."

He lowered his eyes and studied his cup, his mouth tightening into that telltale sign of disapproval. But I went on: "Tonight you're coming with me to the Ritz. If you don't like what you see, then you'll have to find another place to stay. If you accept it, then welcome to New York. I'm living life the way I want to up here. This ain't Carson City, and you'll have to get used to it."

It was a brutal initiation into New York's raunchy gay life but it was the only way we could do it. So that night, my stepbrother saw me not only strip naked before nearly five hundred men, he watched me sucking off two of them in their seats and then getting fucked right there onstage.

When he came to my dressing room, his eyes were wide, his face pale. "Well, baby brother, all I can say is—you work hard for your money." He hugged me. Although he might not approve, he accepted me.

"Welcome to New York," I laughed.

But in bed that night, I knew that in some

important ways, he hadn't changed. My hands explored his heroic body, caressing his pumped-up pecs, his stomach—but when I started to take his erection in my mouth, he covered it with his hands.

"I'm sorry but I still feel the same way. Hands, yes, but mouth, no."

And so, for the first time in four years, I masturbated him several times that night and thought: other men must have done this besides me. And when I asked him the next morning, he smiled. "Well, maybe so. If in the right place and the right time. It seems like guys are always wanting to grope me. Not only my privates, but my butt."

He was drying off from the shower and at that moment put a foot up on a stool, giving me a shimmering picture of white butt jutting out above powerful legs.

"Steve, you have only to look in the mirror to see why."

CHAPTER FOUR

NOVEMBER 24, 1980—9:45 P.M.

Kendell loved everything about his job.

In his metal cage above the mob, he could twist and shake his naked booty and watch the guys jerking off by watching him.

"Shake Your Groove Thing," sang Peaches and Herb, and he went into another wild routine—flipping his cock against the hard metal and rubbing his ass.

Pink Pony was packed because it had finally stopped raining. Thanksgiving was two days away, and already the partying had started. Sweat dripped from Kendell's tanned body, which rippled with muscles. He had worked hard to achieve the taut body so prized by New York gays. His cock was bigger than most, which was the main reason he was hired as one of the ever-popular go-go boys.

There were hundreds of handsome men packed together, but a few caught his eye. There was that handsome older man with the mustache sitting drinking at the bar. He looked like a sea captain. He had been watching Kendell all night, winking and toasting him silently. *Maybe I'll go off with him after I'm finished.* A group of husky college types were grouped together at a table near the wall—big, burly, getting drunk on beer. They, too, had been calling out propositions.

"Come on down and gobble it," one of them had yelled and shook his cock up at Kendell, who made a gobbling motion with his mouth. He could have any of them. But there was a real cutie-pie standing alone against the wall, watching him through dark glasses, now and then smoothing his mustache.

He was bigger than most, with muscles galore. Men had been trying to grope him all night. He seemed the moody kind, though, and that always intrigued Kendell.

"Ring My Bell" sang Anita Ward, and Kendell put on an unusually frenetic jig, rubbing his cock against the metal ribbing, and rubbing his hands into his ass. His work was not ignored for the Sea Captain, the rowdy college kids and the mysterious hunk all watched and applauded when he finished.

George, the bartender helped him down from the cage and handed him a towel. "You look like you just came in from a shower."

"A shower is exactly where I'm heading," laughed Kendell. Have my gin and tonic ready, baby, in ten minutes flat!"

Quickly he showered in the tiny space near the busy tearoom and threw on a gold sweater and tight corduroy slacks. He remembered to put on his dark wig. Even though he felt safe, he didn't want to take any chances with that gay killer on the loose.

George had his drink ready, and Kendell gulped it down. "Mmmm, another. Another, Georgie-boy!"

"Don't get drunk now," warned the cute bartender. "You've got to be careful with that nut on the loose."

The alcohol had already touched his brain for he felt so incredibly good and cute and powerful. Lifting up the edge of his wig, he winked. "I can promise you, Georgie, nobody's getting this cute little slut."

"Kendell!" George warned with a shake of his head as he watched the lounge's most popular dancer gulp down his drink.

He had smoked some grass before the show and

73

now his head felt wonderful—a little woozy, but alert. He knew exactly which trick he would ball with. He went up to the mysterious stranger, who was watching him with a slight smile on his mouth.

"Did you like watching me up there?" Kendell asked, moving close to him and growing even more impressed. Lord, but he was cute. The short, curly hair made his face look so naked and handsome. And those shoulders and chest. His flannel shirt was unbuttoned halfway down so his pecs bulged out like women tits.

"You put on a wild show up there," the man grinned. He spoke softly, with a faint accent. Was it Irish, British? "My name's Roger. I teach English at a high school here."

"Hi, Roger!" Kendell giggled. "My name's Kendell Kramer and I'd love to know you better and see if that bulge in your britches is real."

"You're free to find out." Roger smiled. "Isn't there some place we can go?"

"Back here, back here," Kendell whispered, grabbing his hand and dragging him back to the tiny little dressing room he shared with the other go-go boys. It was empty now.

Kendell fell to his knees, unbuckled Roger, and let out a whoop when he scooped up the abundant privates which overflowed his hand.

"Holy shit, I've hit pay dirt!"

He crammed the soft cock into his mouth, jabbing his tongue into the slit and felt the organ instantly thicken. Within minutes, after furious sucking, he was able to wrap his fists around it and he worked to milk it.

74

Kendell's mouth was flooded unexpectedly with a thick gush of sperm, which whetted his appetite for more of this man's cock. To his amazement, it didn't soften, and he was startled to enjoy another jet of copious semen merely five minutes later.

Gasping for breath, Kendell struggled to his feet, using Roger's large penis as a pulley, and embraced this surprising stud.

They kissed and Kendell was thrilled when this big male fell to his knees, pulled out the dancer's prick, and began sucking. He was terrific and surprising. To Kendell, this guy looked strictly trade: the kind who liked getting done but did nothing in return.

When Kendell ejaculated, the man turned him around and began rimming him. "I've been wanting to fuck you ever since I saw you up there."

Somebody tried to open the door. "Hey, who's in there? Kendell, I need to get in and shower."

"Just a sec, dahling, I'm coming out. Go get a beer and be back in five minutes. I'll be finished."

"Oh, okay, I get it. Enjoy."

Kendell smiled. "That's our private code, when we're tricking with one of the guys."

Roger still had his hands on Kendell's ass and groaned, "Let me fuck you! Isn't there some other place?"

"Well, I dunno. I'm staying at the Hudnutt Apartment Building with a roommate. He's gone to Fire Island this weekend. I promised not to bring anybody home. You know, the gay killer and all—"

"Fuck the killer! I'm not, and so that's that.

Let's go. You've never been fucked until you've had me drilling you."

"Roger, do you promise me, do you swear you won't do anything dangerous? I'm trusting you."

"I swear to God, I'm harmless. Okay? Good. Now let me leave first. I came with another guy and if he sees us leaving together—"

"Meet me outside across the street. There's an alleyway, and —"

Roger was even more luscious without his shirt. Kendell sucked the thick nipples and then moved his lips down the stranger's chest.

"Wait. Let's get on the bed and let me start fucking. You wanna make me hard first, though, don't you?"

Kendell had pulled open the buttons on the tight jeans and crammed his mouth again over Roger's sticky cock. Once again it rose up fast, but before he could taste its delicious contents, Roger picked him up easily and carried him to the bed.

Milly, Kendell's black cat, meowed and jumped up onto the dresser where they had placed a six-pack of Bud. Roger clicked open a can and gave it to Kendell.

"Strip naked, baby, and let me see what I saw up in the cage."

"You'll see more than that, Roger. Look!" Kendell ripped off his brown wig and threw it into the corner. "See? I've been wearing this stupid wig because that killer only goes for blonds. See my golden curls? Ain't they purty?"

"I knew you were blonde." Roger smiled. "I've

seen you dance before. Turn over on your stomach now. I can't wait much longer."

"My roomie would kill me if he knew I'd brought you or anybody home," Kendell giggled. "He says I'm too reckless and I trust people too easily. But with you, I have this sixth sense that told me I could trust you."

He looked over his shoulder. Roger had his back turned and was staring at him over his shoulder. Why didn't he take off his jeans?

"Hurry up, Roger! Let's get it on. Take your damned pants off."

He watched the muscular man peel off the thin denim and was curious to see the black circle around his waist, beneath the waistband of the skivvies.

"What's that? A black belt?"

"It keeps my waistline from getting beyond a thirty-four. Now just close your eyes and you're gonna feel like Christmas."

Kendell obeyed, but not before draining some more of his beer. God, it tasted bitter. He shouldn't have smoked that pot earlier.

He shivered in delight as he felt Roger's tongue drive up into his butthole. His hands were so warm and soft. Already he was growing hard.

The bed creaked as Roger got on and Kendell felt the fingers tapping his opening and then—there was a sharp blow down there. Before he could flip over, the pain was so horrible that he curled up.

Cloth—Roger's underwear—was thrust into his mouth and as he looked down, he saw the bed turning scarlet—from the blood gushing from his anus.

77

Looking up, he watched Roger, smilingly and casually, bring the straight razor up again to slice into his scrotum. Before he could scream silently, the leather rope came off Roger's waist and encircled the go-go boy's neck.

CHAPTER FIVE

"Help Me! Before I kill again! All perverts must be wiped out!"

Together, Steve and I watched the TV screen, where a bulletin had interrupted *Mayberry, RFD* with Andy Griffith.

"This was the anonymous note sent to the *New*

York Post this morning, along with a lock of hair which police say belongs to that of the latest gay murder victim" intoned the grim-faced TV reporter. "Again, Kendell Kramer, a go-go dancer at the Pink Pony Lounge, a popular hangout for gay men, was found hanging in his apartment at the Hudnutt Apartment Building last night. He was brutally mutilated in the same form as the other victims, all of whom were gay strippers and dancers."

"Jesus!" Steve muttered, turning the channel to an old rerun of *I Love Lucy*. "This time it happened less than ten blocks from here."

"Well, we'll be out of here by Christmas," I sighed. "Maybe we can get a guarded cell at Rikers Island."

Steve grabbed my shoulders and shook me. "You don't know what a sitting duck you are, little brother! You don't see how those guys look at you up here, bareassed, or worse still, getting fucked or sucked off right there on stage."

He was getting on my nerves and I couldn't resist a taunt. "Why worry? I've got that big, strong Irishman down the hall to protect me."

I knew how much Sam O'Brien got on Steve's nerves and watched him erupt. "That guy's an animal! I was coming in while ago from jogging, and his door was cracked open. I heard all this moaning and groaning. I peeked in and there he was, getting fucked by that black security guard."

I doubled over, laughing. It sounded like Sam. I wondered if he hadn't set the whole thing up just to get under Steve's skin.

"Steve, don't you know an exhibitionist when you see one? He loves an audience! I'm surprised he hasn't joined the Ritz. He certainly got everyone's cocks standing up when he did it with me."

Steve grimaced. "You won't be laughing if he turns out to be the killer. When you see him, just ask him where he's been for the past two days."

Steve picked up his duffel and hurried away. He had a modeling assignment that morning for a Macy's catalog spread. They wanted him as one of their bathing-suit studs.

As soon as Steve left, though, I hurried to Sam's room. As usual, the door was cracked open, and I could hear Sam's laughter.

When I looked in, I laughed again. Sam was lying, in bed naked as usual. A towel was wrapped around his cock. With drink in hand, he was snickering with one of the other security guards, a big, husky black kid named Leroy.

"Sam, what in the hell happened? You look like you really tied one on!"

He grinned but then moaned, clasping his head and putting down his glass of liquor. "Oh, Jesus, beautiful, you'll never believe what all's happened to me."

"Tell him," Leroy hooted, rubbing himself. He wore just the pants of his guard uniform, and he looked like the rough type that Sam enjoyed.

"I was at the Adonis Theater last night," Sam muttered, squeezing the towel, "and I stuck my cock in this glory hole. The guys were lined up waiting to suck me. But I got so swollen, I couldn't get it out. Thank God Leroy saved the day."

"I found this guy who had a jar of Vaseline."
Leroy grinned. "We rubbed it over Sam's cock
here, and that's how he got it out of the glory
hole. Let him see it, Sam."

When Sam pulled the towel away, I whistled.
Other than looking swollen to nearly twice its
size, it was a glorious red with the tip the size of a
small apple.

"You need some lotion on that," I said. "Let me
get my Nivea. It'll make it feel great."

"Anything!" Sam moaned. "Oooh, it feels like
it's on fire."

I returned quickly with my trusty bottle of
Nivea and began slathering it on Sam's swollen
balls. "And to top it all off," Sam complained, "this
black stud began fucking me after we got back
here, which didn't help."

"You wanted my cock up your ass," Leroy
protested. "When I got it up there, you didn't
want it out."

"Look at my butthole, Brett," Sam said. "It
feels like it's on fire, too."

He pulled his legs back, and Leroy came to see,
too. Other than a luscious pink hue, his ass
looked beautiful. Leroy rubbed himself.

"Mmm, I'm getting hard just looking at it."

"And I think what Sam needs here is a good
blowjob," I grinned.

"Hey, what're you two plotting?" Sam demand-
ed. I wrapped my hands around his swollen organ
and began licking the tip. Leroy grunted his
admiration. I heard his pants hitting the floor.
Then I slipped more of Sam's erection into my

mouth. Sam winced, but then his face settled into an expression of rapture.

"Yeah, yeah, that's what I need! Just a blowjob by an expert."

Leroy positioned himself between Sam's thighs. I was amazed at the length of his dark cock— long, slightly curved, it resembled a dildo.

I paused to watch him pop his tip up into the butthole. Sam grunted and Leroy carefully pushed the rest of it up until just his balls hung outside. Using my hands, I began stroking Sam's dark hard-on. And although he grimaced and rolled his eyes, I sensed he was thrilled with the painful but exhilarating feeling of getting both blown and fucked at the same time.

Suddenly thick gobs of white spurted across his stomach. Leroy sped up his hip movements, and I got behind to watch him fucking. He was brutal, withdrawing his prick all the way and then mashing it back into the moist hole. Sam whooped, gasped, but begged him to continue.

Finally the black guard pulled out and scooted up to cram the hard-on into Sam's mouth. He gagged, his face turned purple but he swallowed furiously as the load pumped into his throat. He didn't take it out, either.

He flipped Leroy over on his back and began blowing him passionately. I didn't have time to watch any longer. I had a busy morning ahead of me. But as I closed the door, I saw Sam's head bobbing hungrily over Leroy's long, slender cock.

What a priest he must have made! I smiled. I

couldn't imagine him controlling his libido in the confines of a church.

My visit with Sam had taken my mind briefly off the realities of living in New York.

But I had to brave the freezing cold and wind all morning, for I simply had to find a new apartment. I had only four weeks left before the landlord would close down my studio. And there was that chilling new murder to cause me to glance over my shoulder continually as I hurried to the subway.

I clutched the circled apartment ads from the Sunday *Times* and checked off the first one. "Cozy, bachelor pad with RV VU." It turned out to be a hole in the wall on 12th Street with garbage-strewn hallways and a baby screaming.

In another nearby vacancy, "a gem for the single person," the corridors smelled of frying fish and cigars. The only people I saw were the elderly, hobbling around with walkers and canes.

Rain was falling again as I grabbed some groceries at Sloan's and prepared to cross the street. It was then I saw the stranger again. Dark glasses hid his eyes; ratty-looking hair curled around his shoulders. He was watching me from a corner of the grocery store.

When he saw me watching him, he grinned and ducked back behind the building.

In the lobby of the Vanderbilt Arms, I was relieved to see Sam and Leroy in their guard uniforms, chatting with one of the elderly residents.

"Sam, there was some creep up over there at Sloan's watching me. I've seen him before."

Both he and Leroy looked out at the rain-soaked scene, but it was too misty to make out very much. Sam went with me to the elevator. "I'll go with you to your apartment."

In the elevator, he rubbed himself. "Um, mm, I'm giving my little fellow a rest. It's become overworked."

"Sam, forget your cock for a minute. That guy I saw gives me the creeps."

"It's just that whenever I'm around you, I keep thinking of how great your cock tasted when I sucked it at the Ritz, and how wonderful your ass felt when I fucked you.

"There will be other occasions, I'm sure." I smiled. "Thanks for coming up."

I locked the door and flew around the place, putting some soup into the crockpot for Steve and then dashed into the shower. I was running late again but I made sure I had my "weapons" in place. I had hidden a screwdriver behind the toilet just in case someone broke in.

As I bathed, I suddenly froze. I turned off the water. I had heard the distinct sound of a door closing.

"Steve?"

No answer. Alert now, I threw on my robe and grabbed the screwdriver. I could see the rest of the studio from the narrow hallway. No one was there, unless he was hiding behind the counter separating the kitchen from the rest of the room.

It, too, was empty.

The bed. It looked—different. I had made it up neatly, as I usually did, with the leopard-spotted pillows on the black-and-gold comforter. But now there was something else there.

A male doll with golden hair lay there with its arms stretched out to me. Around its neck was a black cord. Attached was a note: HELP ME BEFORE I STRIKE AGAIN!

Chapter Six

Detective Ramon Rivera was a big, swarthy detective with the NYPD. His partner, Butch Jerrigan, was husky and brown-haired with impish blue eyes.

They had me reenact where I was when I heard the door closing and then what happened next. But my stepbrother wasn't helping things with his near-hysteria.

"For God's sake, you've had him do it four times!" Steve cried, rubbing his hands against his jeans. He had rushed home as soon as I told him what had happened.

"Please, please," Detective Rivera grumped, "would you just calm down some? We need to get this down straight."

Sam and Leroy leaned against the kitchen counter, smoking, looking grim. Somehow someone had gotten past them and come up to my room, and somehow the intruder had managed to pick the lock and get inside. If I had been killed...

Both had alibis for that time period. Old Mrs. Kroger had needed their assistance to get some groceries from a taxi, which had taken only a few minutes.

"But she was the only person to see them," Steve blurted out. "She's senile. She doesn't know when this happened."

"Please, please," Butch grunted. "You're holding up progress. We understand your concern, pal."

When he asked us both to come down to the precinct and fill out a report, I was relieved to get out of the building.

But when we got there, I was startled when both detectives studied me.

"This Sam O'Brien, the security guard. We've got a file on him. I didn't want to make it too obvious with him there," Butch Jernigan said.

"See?" Steve cried triumphantly. "What did I tell you?"

"Well, it's hardly anything life-threatening." Detective Rivera headed to a cabinet and leafed through a number of files. Pulling one out, he came back and grinned.

"Seems like this Mr. Sam O'Brien has been picked up a few times for public lewdness. Like—getting-gang banged in Central Park. Like—sucking off college boys in Grand Central Station. Like, parading around bareassed at the Adonis movie theater."

"Ha, that sounds like Sam!" I laughed. "So what? All that stuff is harmless."

"You say you dance at the Ritz?" Butch put in. "There's another dancer you might keep your eye on. Bruno. He's got a pretty hot rap sheet."

"Not the Bruno I know!" I gasped. "He's got a dark reputation, but that's mostly show-biz puff."

"Oh, no," Butch filled me in. Taking out another file, he read to me a chilling history: Bruno, son of wealthy Texas oil people, had spent two years in a mental hospital after threatening to murder his prep-school headmaster. He had been involved in a satanic cult in Houston and had been expelled from college for threatening to murder a boyfriend.

"Well, so what?" I repeated. "He's always okay around me."

"It's just that we have him under surveillance as a possible suspect in the gay killings. He uses a leather rope in his act. He likes to don disguises, we understand. He vanishes for days at a time."

They told me to be on my guard more than

ever. The doll was an obvious sign that I was being watched by someone who wanted to do me harm.

On the way out, Rivera grinned. "Say, I hear you put on a really hot show at the Ritz. Taking off your clothes and making the guys feel real nice."

"Sure," I smiled. "That's my job. Come by tonight, and I'll have you a ticket for you and your buddy there. It's going to be a really wild show because it's Thanksgiving."

"Me?" Ramon mocked, putting a hand to his mouth. "I'm married with two kids."

"Don't listen to him." Butch laughed. "If it's got to do with sex, my friend here loves it."

"If you come, then sit close to the walkway that goes out into the theater. And be sure and leave your inhibitions at home."

Steve stayed close to me as we both hurried to the Ritz. He had agreed to strip on Amateur Night for the $500. But he wanted to discuss with Matt Dempsey the second part—of losing his virginity publicly. All my fears of the doll incident was pushed aside. Excitement filled me for Thanksgiving night was one of our biggest events of the year.

CHAPTER SEVEN

As Steve and I dashed along Broadway to the Ritz, I couldn't dwell on death and danger. A powerful surge of vibrant life along Times Square struck everyone that clear, freezing night.

At the Show Palace, there was their answer to Thanksgiving: a "turkey gobble" onstage along with a $100 Amateur Strip Night.

At the raunchy little Ramrod, a free Thanks-giving buffet was available to all its customers while on stage, there were "Broadway's Biggest Boys." Critics might accuse this bouncy, lively theater of being sleazy, but there was an unmistakable ambiance of comaraderie among the dancers and their fans.

The 55th Street Playhouse was packed for its holiday double feature: *Private Collection,* plus *Sex Magic* with the superhung Roger.

The Kings was showing three old classics: Johnny Dawes in *Bad, Bad Boys* and *Los Bandidos,* with its cast of sultry Latino jailbait.

I was tempted to drop into one of my favorite spots, the Gaiety which was featuring a "dynamite marathon with 12 boys and the Apollo Room—where Boy Meets Boy!" Among their star strippers that night were Jack, Damon, Fernando, and Joshua, and the movies also looked tempting: *Lusty Burglar* and *Sex Pack*.

Even before we entered the Ritz, where men were lined up in the cold, shivering in their leather jackets with fur collars, we could hear Kool and the Gang bouncing the audience inside with "Celebration," one of the most popular hits at all the discos that November.

It was like one, big party that night. More than a hundred men were enjoying the lavish complimentary buffet catered all night from the corner Howard Johnson. Roy, the cowboy from Texas, was onstage, naked except for his cowboy hat, and had tied one end of rope to his cock and was throwing it out to some lucky man in the jammed theater. The recipient of the lasso would tug gently, and Roy would mosey on down and sit in his lap and the patron could do anything he wanted.

Grabbing Steve's hand, I led him up to the rear of the second floor where Matt Dempsey kept his opulent office. Like an old-time theatrical impresario, he loved the good life and you saw it instantly when you walked into his thickly carpeted office.

He had a window that looked directly out on the crowd and the stage. With just a glance, he could tell which dancers were winning the audience and which ones wouldn't be asked to return. Roy had been followed onstage by Marcel, a prissy ballet type who had made it clear he was "only slumming for money" by stripping there. As he went into his bloodless poses and wriggled his butt, Matt looked up at us, made a gesture toward the elegant performer and drew a finger across his neck. Marcel was finished there.

Matt poured us champagne into heavy crystal goblets, offered us some appetizers from a side table, and with china plates loaded with chilled shrimp, cheeses, and stuffed mushrooms, we discussed Steve's debut.

"I'll accept your offer about taking off my clothes," my stepbrother said. "But on that second part—about, uh, getting fucked and sucked onstage, I don't know."

Matt smiled seductively and pulled out his check ledger. With a flourish, he filled out the check but before handing it to Steve, he picked up a pair of scissors and cut it in two. He gave Steve one.

"There," Matt said, "you've got half a thousand dollars. If you go through with the sex, you'll get the other half."

"Wait a minute, Matt!" I interrupted. "That ain't fair. I don't want Steve to feel like he's got to have sex. To you and me, it's no big deal. There's more fucking and sucking on the stage of the Ritz in one night than most men experience in a year."

Matt shrugged his broad shoulders and settled back into his leather chair, lighting up a Marlboro. "No one's forced to do anything here. You think about it, son. I don't want anyone to ever accuse me of forcing them to have sex here."

As we got up to leave, Matt protested. "Hey, if I'm paying you all this money, Steve, couldn't you let me see what I'm getting?"

My stepbrother smiled, shrugged, and did a natural striptease that would have given any crowd throbbing hard-ons. His cheeks still pink from the cold, he removed his leather jacket, red muffler, and work boots. Then stripping off his black turtleneck, he let his loose khaki slacks fall to the floor, so that he stood only in his white B.V.D.s.

"These, too?" He ran his fingers beneath his waistband.

"Those, too," Matt laughed.

Steve peeled them off and in the soft gold lighting, his muscles glowing, his cock hanging heavy, with the foreskin half-shrouding the tip, he looked fantastic.

"Oh, Jesus!" Matt said lightly, pretending to fan himself. "You'll bring the house down! Turn around, Mr. Adonis. Bulge those muscles, baby!"

He obeyed, letting Matt get a look at his high-mounted rump. Matt pretended to collapse in his chair.

"If you did just that onstage, the guys would be creaming all over the joint. If you had real sex, we'd have to call in the paramedics. Okay, you've shown me my hunch is right. On Christmas Eve, I want you here, on my stage."

"Get your britches on, Steve," I laughed, "I'm about due onstage and I've got a new outfit."

Outside the office, I hugged Steve and kissed him. "Honey, you were fantastic. And please, for my sake, do not go through with this sex crap. I know you don't want to do it. We don't need the money."

"I'll think about it," he said thoughtfully. "I'll be watching you. Knock'em dead."

"I'll knock *you* dead if you're expecting something respectful. It'll be wild. You can see what I'll be getting into. Don't worry. I'm changing."

As I hurried to backstage, I thought: he's right. In some ways he is getting more mellow. A small-town hunk comes to Babylon-on-the-Hudson, discovers his stepbrother is a stripper and sex performer, and now he's preparing to follow in his footsteps—all in just three months? Yes, Steve has come a long way.

It was crazy backstage. A party was going on. Matt had set up our own lavish buffet table, with endless champagne. I passed by the arrogant Marcel, who was angrily throwing his "costume"—some beads and sequins—into his duffel and yelling: "Ha, they think by firing me I'm upset. I wouldn't work in this fucking shithole another second. You're nothing but animals."

Roy, still naked and his cock glistening from the blowjob his lassoed admirer had given him, made a mooing sound. Pepe, who hadn't yet sucked his own cock that night, made chicken noises. Bruno, clad all in leather, made flipping motions with his wrist.

"Oh, Miss Thing jus' needs to be understood. She's such a brilliant dancer! Go back to the fucking New York Ballet, bitch!"

I grabbed a bottle of champagne and glass and fled to my dressing room. I had only a few minutes to get dolled up. When I emerged, the others screeched and applauded.

That night, inspired by my encounter with the NYPD that afternoon, I had gotten out a new outfit I planned to wear New Year's. I was dressed like a cop.

Peering through the curtains, my eyes scanned the crowd. God, there must've been hundreds and hundreds. Men were lined up against the wall, some sitting two to a seat. Several had stripped naked, and in the darker corners, I could make out swiveling head motions over the lap of a neighbor.

I laughed when I saw the big figure of Sam O'Brien, sitting barebutt close to the wooden ramp. A man's head was lowered over my neighbor's spread thighs. And two rows down were the familiar faces of my detective buddies: Ramon Rivera and Butch Jernigan.

They were so cute and macho that Teddy, the Surfer Boy, was writhing close to their faces. The detectives grinned, and when the dancer offered them his cock, they laughed and shook their heads.

"I'm going to change all that," I muttered and prepared myself.

Tonight I had chosen another old R&B classic: "Sixty-Minute Man" by The Dominoes. When I came out in my dark glasses, tight britches, and cop hat, the crowd shouted and roared their approval. My cop buddies threw their heads back and howled.

I swiveled and shook, whirled my glasses around and within minutes my law-enforcement facade lay scattered around the stage as I began slinking slowly down the walkway, winking and laughing at my two new buddies.

Ramon pretended to pray while Butch was impishly pointing toward his buddy's cock which was hanging half-erect out of his pants.

"I rock 'em, roll 'em, all night," sang the Sixty-Minute Man of the song. I fell to my stomach and crawled closer to Ramon, who pretended to cover his eyes and slid down in his seat. But when he looked up, his dark eyes were hot and his grin inviting.

From the walkway, I crawled down into his lap, stretching my legs over to Butch, rubbing my privates against Ramon's chest. Butch began rubbing his hands over my thighs, squeezing my butt. My cock began rising.

Ramon glanced from that sight to Butch, who had pushed his britches down to his ankle so I could feel his thickening erection.

"Suck it, Mr. Detective," I cooed. "Make it feel good."

Ramon lowered his head and took all of my hard-on. Sweat was sparkling on his face, but his mouth was hot and hungry. Butch pushed his mouth up to my groin and licked it, and then Ramon gave him my dick.

Back and forth they shared it until finally I couldn't hold it back anymore. I warned them and they drew back so all the others, panting and drooling, could see their reward. I came big—several strong spurts—which was too much for Ramon. He turned me around, stood up and began edging his dick up into my ass.

Butch crawled around to get in front of me and stuck my dick into his mouth again. The crowd was thrilled to see these butch-looking guys flipping out over me. Ramon was a skilled, passionate fucker and he came within minutes. It felt so good, I shot once more, too, with Butch taking it all.

All this had lasted only a little more than fifteen minutes with the song throbbing along with the action. By the time I kissed my two partners, grabbed my clothes, and bounded back behind the curtains, the entire theater had become overheated with lust. I peered back out through the curtains and saw my two new lovers slumped in their chairs, smiling happily as people around them slapped their shoulders and complimented them on their "routines."

Then I saw my stepbrother among the men lining the wall. He stood out even in his regular clothes, but his expression was different from the others. While the others were laughing, joking, and whispering, his reaction was strange. He was glaring at my two detective friends. Suddenly he turned and left.

"What's your stepbrother so upset for?" Teddy had been watching the scene with me. His cock was slimy from having been sucked and brushed against my leg.

"Who knows and who cares?" I drawled. "Tonight I worry about no one else except little ole me! Hey, where's me drink? I think I'll get loaded."

"Now, you're talking!" Teddy laughed. We joined the others, who were getting sappy on the unlimited champagne. Even Bruno had broken out of character and was acting sociable.

He came up to me in his leather uniform and stared into my eyes. His were dark and glittering from either too much drink or drugs. But then rumor had it that he hated drugs because his younger brother had overdosed on them.

"You put on quite a show tonight, Mr. Cop." He smiled. "When you were getting sucked and fucked, you made me come."

"I'm highly flattered. Are you trying to tell me something? I've heard you've got a most colorful past."

His face shadowed. "Oh, the cops must have talked to you. They visited me together—about the murders."

"Look, dahling, if it'll make you feel any better, I told them I trusted you. You could never do anything like that."

His expressive little-boy face lightened and he

99

leaned forward to kiss me. "I was hoping you would. Now may I ask if you'd consider being my partner for the Christmas show? Matt thinks it'd be a smash hit. You've got your fans, I've got mine. If they saw us both together, wow—think of the possibilities!"

Just then, Matt came up to us. "Has Bruno mentioned his idea to you? What do you say? I think it would knock everybody out of their fucking seats to see you doing it."

"Let me catch my breath. It'd be dynamite. Because, mainly, I've always wanted to ball with you, beautiful. And it would be fun doing it before a crowd."

Matt leaned closer to us. "If you do, I'll give you a bonus that'll have you laughing all the way to the bank."

"Let's do it!" I laughed and Bruno, trying to keep a grin from his usually serious face, moved closer and kissed me, guiding my hand down to his crotch.

"In that case, you'd better get familiar with this and me with yours."

I agreed to visit him at his Village loft for our first "rehearsal" in a week. Word spread quickly among the other dancers. They were amazed—and delighted. Bruno had never had any of the dancers as his prized "duo." It was always someone from the audience or one of his rough buddies.

But not everyone was so thrilled. Pepe, the Mexican hunk, came up to me later and whispered, "Honey, do you think you're doing the right thing? I mean, Bruno's gorgeous but he's got a reputation! He's safe onstage, but in private? You'd better take some protection along, or else let somebody know where you are."

Matt took me home in his chauffeured limousine long after midnight. In the thick cushions of the backseat, we sipped more champagne. He loved taking off my clothes. When I was naked, he sucked my nipples and then moved his mouth down to my privates.

I didn't think I could do anything more since I had had more hot action during my second appearance. But I came abundantly. As I left Matt's limousine, he repeated the same warning as Pepe: "This thing with Bruno: just keep in mind what kind of a guy he is. He's a great lay. I should know. But he's kinky. You let me know what hours you're at his place because anything can happen."

Steve was already curled up asleep when I stepped into the apartment.

I poured a glass of milk and took it to the window. Below, the traffic streamed by in the city that never sleeps. No one moved around, though.

Then I saw the figure standing across the street in the dim neon sign of the Sloan's supermarket. Long hair fell to his broad shoulders. Even though it was night, he wore dark glasses. They were trained right on me. I moved back, but he glided away, like someone who wasn't human.

PART III

The Final Curtain

"The gay community has reason to be furious with the inept reaction to the series of unsolved gay murders by city officials and especially the NYPD. Although police have a special unit whose sole purpose is to solve the slaying of four gay strippers, not one clue has been turned up. And in the meantime, there is this terrible sense of doom hanging over New York's homosexuals that there is no doubt the maniac is quite probably plotting his next attack. It isn't a good time to be blond, good-looking, and strip at any of the Big Apple's gay hangouts."

—Editorial in the *Village Voice*
December 20, 1980

Chapter Eight

The night after Bruno and I agreed to perform our sexual duo onstage at the Ritz, word began to spread through the gay world of Manhattan and consequently into the gossip columns.

Thanks to Matt Dempsey's genius at exploitation, spicy little ads began appearing in the *Village*

Voice, showing mug shots of Bruno and me smiling sexily above the blurb:

THE TWO HOTTEST GAY STARS IN THE BUSINESS!
TOGETHER, NUDE, LIVE
CHRISTMAS EVE NIGHT!
ONLY AT THE RITZ MALE FOLLIES!

The telephones began ringing off the hook because our fans wanted to make reservations. A huge new poster was erected above our marquee. I was shown in just a bikini, staring over at Bruno, who wore just a leather jacket that barely covered his butt, with cigarette dangling from his lips. THEY'LL DO IT LIVE!

ONSTAGE, FOR ONE NIGHT ONLY! DOING WHAT THEY DO BEST! DECEMBER 24TH!

The ads and exploitation were daring, but in great taste—slick, sensual, blunt, but hinting at fantastic sights.

While Matt was having a ball watching our fans' interest build, I was hurtling through each day like someone shot out of a cannon.

Living in Manhattan has been described as everything from existing on the rim of an exploding volcano to surviving in a concrete jungle. To me, it was as if I were on one of these exercise treadmills that had gone haywire and I couldn't get off.

My life was changing dramatically, as was the lives of the ones I loved. It was only another week before Steve and I had to move out of the Vanderbilt Arms.

He looked, I looked for the perfect place. Matt suggested we both move in with him at his extravagant suite at the Plaza Hotel, but we didn't want any ties or obligations. Matt would have attached strings to both of us. Steve would certainly not want that type of ménage à trois.

Finally we found the perfect studio on swanky Riverside Drive—a cozy cocoon on the tenth floor, with a gorgeous view of the Hudson River, a small park beneath us, a fireplace.

We could sublet it until spring for just $500. We snatched it up. I wanted something more swinging, but this would do for the cold wintry months.

My relationship with Detectives Rivera and Butch had evolved into more than just frequent sessions of hot sex in some of the hotel rooms the city rented for prospective witnesses in criminal cases.

They arranged for me to get a licensed gun and taught me how to shoot it at a firing range. And when they heard I was going to meet Bruno at his place for "rehearsals" of our public coupling, they expressed their uneasiness.

"If you ever go to his place, you let us know," Ramon warned. "We hear some weird things go on in that loft of his. At least two cases of missing boys placed them at his place the night before they vanished."

And when Steve heard me joke about going to Bruno's much talked-about loft, he was aghast.

"The hell you're going there!" he sputtered. "If you go, I'm going along."

Actually, Bruno put everyone's minds to rest when he met with me in my dressing room a few days after our agreement and after the publicity was launched.

"You know what I suggest we do?" He smiled strangely. "I think that if we're going to really have the hots for each other onstage, we shouldn't touch each other until then."

I was sitting at my dressing table, dabbing on some mascara for my routine. My mouth fell open. "You're shitting me, Bruno! I thought that by, well, you know, doing some balling might help us get used to each other."

Just then, Matt dropped by to show us the ads and overheard my response. He surprised me by agreeing with Bruno.

"He's right, you beautiful little slut. Get yourselves all sexed up over each other, and don't do anything until you're on that stage. Choreograph your movements, pick out the music, but just don't fucking do it."

Bruno calmly lit up a Salem. "What I had in mind is for us to watch each other balling with others. Seeing how we respond—that could really make our temperatures rise for each other."

He surprised me when he asked me if I would bring Sam O'Brien along as a partner.

"He lives just down the hall from you, doesn't he? He was the best sucker and fucker I've ever balled with!"

I hooted. "Oh, God, he'll be thrilled when I ask him. Sex is his favorite thing."

Matt cut in, "Say, if you three are getting together, isn't it a good time to break your stepbrother in, Brett? I don't know how you two are planning this, but we don't want him to freak out onstage when he gets sucked and fucked."

"Steve still hasn't decided about that part," I said firmly. "Matt, I thought I made it clear, I'm not forcing my stepbrother to do something this radical! I know Steve! You don't know what a horrible time he had with gay sex because of our lousy stepfather."

Matt held up his hand. "Please, don't give me the spill about him being sexually abused and that destroyed him. Lots of gay guys were raped or beaten up as kids, but they survived. Now Look at these ads. In the one next week, I..."

But what I didn't tell them was that it was Steve who was now insisting he was ready to do it onstage." He had blurted this out the night before after a frustrating day of auditions for commercials and stage rolès that never seemed to come through.

He was being laid off from his spa job after Christmas because of the recession. It seemed nothing had worked out for him since coming to New York.

"Steve, why did you leave your coaching job down south to come up here? Surely, you knew it was going to be tough?"

"I didn't want to get stuck in a small-town rut," he sighed. "People have always told me how great I looked, especially you. So, maybe if I let loose at the Ritz, it could change things."

I brought him his hot Ovaltine as he studied the

TV screen which was showing Joan Crawford walking out into an ocean, wearing a black sequined dress, to meet death in one of our favorite movies, *Humoresque.*

"Once more," I began, rubbing his neck, "you aren't cut out for this crap at the Ritz. Me, I love it. It's natural. For you—"

He put his steaming mug down and hugged me. "It'll only be for an hour. I can handle getting fucked again. God knows Stepdaddy did it to me enough to show me I can do it. In just an hour I can make another $500, and that'll give us $1,000."

I sighed and we went to bed, but his sleep was troubled that night. He twitched and moaned from some disturbing dream. Once I heard him whispering something. I moved my face closer and listened as he muttered, "Not right—evil—evil—"

When I told him I was going to Bruno's loft the next afternoon, along with an hysterically happy Sam O'Brien, I was relieved when Steve replied, "This is incredible. Either of these guys could be the killer. I'm going with you."

"It's going to be wild, O brother of mine!"

"Then so much the better. I'd better see up close what I'll be getting myself in for at the Ritz."

I also phoned my detectives. They insisted that I listen carefully to their directions.

"You're stepping into a mine field," Butch predicted bluntly. "One false step, and it and you could blow up."

On the subway and along the busy sidewalks of West Houston Street, we three men attracted plenty of attention.

Sam, with his blazing red hair, powerful build, and laughing, joking personality, made everyone stare. His leather jacket, tight jeans, and boots emphasized his sensual, hedonistic spirit. He also brazenly gulped steadily from a wine bottle hidden in a paper sack.

And Steve resembled a luscious Clark Gable, packed with muscles, and lacking only the mustache. He wore a white down jacket, snug khakis, and desert boots. He, too, could have been a poster boy or my bodyguard.

For they towered on either side of me, obviously looking after me. Several cute cabbies and messenger boys, and pizza guys from behind their steam-clouded window, winked at me. Matt Dempsey had given me an expensive fringed suede jacket with matching fringed boots as an early Christmas present. A cowboy hat of the same material and a gold scarf fluttering in the wind imbued me with a dash of old Hollywood glamour.

"Are you sure of the address?" Steve asked as we turned into a narrow street littered with wine and beer bottles and an occasional bum.

We looked at the map. "The Savoy Hotel on the corner and now this street. He said 312 West Houston. Hey, here we are."

Sam buzzed the button and Bruno answered: "Okay, guys, come on up. Fifth floor."

The door was buzzed open and we stepped into a

scuzzy little hallway and then an even scuzzier freight elevator. But when we stepped off onto the fifth-floor landing, we all whistled our amazement.

Bruno was there, nude, except for a G-string and biker's hat, all oiled up and mockingly posed as a bodybuilder. But he was in a setting straight out of *Architectural Digest*.

A chandelier sparkled above and beneath his bare feet was a priceless Persian carpet.

"Hey, what bank did you rob to get this joint?" joked Sam, who went up to him and hugged him.

Bruno laughed and dropped his pose. "It *does* help if you've got parents in Texas who own a coupla oil wells, and it doesn't hurt when they send you fat little checks each month. Come on, hunks. I'll show you around."

But before moving, he came over to Steve and me and blew me a kiss. "See? I didn't forget my promise to Matt! I'm not touching you physically until the big night. And you, Adonis? Are you still an untouchable?"

"I may surprise you," grinned Steve who surprised me when he didn't resist a French kiss from Bruno.

"Wooo!" gasped the sultry stripper. "If the rest of your routine is as good as that kiss, you might knock me and Brett off the stage."

His elaborate bar glittered with rows of liquor bottles and stacks of crystal goblets. A stained-glass window filtered in rays of crimson, azure, and gold light. We were delighted when a lion cub ran toward us.

"This is my lil' ole Lambchop! I could be arrested

for having a lion cub, but a rich buddy of mine gave him to me for Thanksgiving and who could refuse?"

We all teased the adorable little creature that nibbled on our fingers and was something Bruno obviously adored. In his private gym, an old-fashioned Wurlitzer jukebox glowed in the corner. All the latest hits were available.

Bruno punched his theme song from the Ritz, Chic's hypnotic version of "Good Times." Bopping and shaking his body, he beckoned us into another room.

We stepped into a chamber straight from the diaries of the Marquis de Sade. Hanging from the ceiling were life-sized mannequins and blow-up dolls. Both sexes were represented and were very anatomically correct.

Big velvet cushions were placed in the corners of the room where dramatic lighting dappled pink and gold shadows onto the black shag carpeting. A smaller bar glowed in the corner. Steve and I accepted cold beer while Sam poured himself a large glass of straight whiskey. Bruno settled for champagne.

As our eyes grew use to the dimness, Sam headed straight to a section of the wall covered with dildos—of every shape and material. Small ones for tight buttholes, enormous ones that could have passed for arms crowned with fists.

Next to them were whips—some were single cords, others had lashes knotted with metal studs. Bruno turned a knob on the wall, and "Good Times" throbbed through the air which was rich with cherry incense.

113

Bruno had moved up to Sam and was removing his clothes. Sam, smiling in anticipation, stood still, waiting, waiting.

"Bruno, where's the pissery?" I asked. "Don't do anything until I get back!"

"Down the hall, second door on the right."

Steve had settled on a cushion and had removed his jacket and sweater. He started to accompany me but I motioned him to stay there.

I passed by a bedroom—it was done completely in black and gold—ebony bed linen, pillows, a gold lamp burning on a nightstand, and the faint metallic scent of a chemical.

The bathroom was done completely in red marble. From the sunken tub, the thick towels, the crystal jars containing bath crystals and oils, all was scarlet. Quickly, I pulled back the crimson curtains and raised the window.

I saw the dusty car parked below, beneath some old trees. The interior was too dark to see, but a hand flashed out of the window. Butch and Ramon were down there. If I didn't return to the window within half an hour, they would know I was in trouble.

In the orgy room, I was startled to find my stepbrother naked except for his white skivvies, watching a very naked Bruno sucking furiously on Sam's thick hard-on.

I felt strange not flinging off my clothes—but I had vowed to my stepbrother, to Sam and to Matt, that I wouldn't even touch Bruno's body until the big night.

I settled down with my beer and thoroughly

114

enjoyed this private show, but I didn't forget to glance at my watch. In thirty minutes, back to the john.

Sam had pushed Bruno down on his back and mounted him. His dark cock bent double as he tried to cram it up into the greedy stripper. When he did, Bruno cried out, "That's it! Oh, do it, rough, rough! Bust my asshole, Sammy!"

Sam humped harder, bringing Bruno's hips up until he was almost standing on his head. His cock was vicious as it plunged brutally in and out of the squealing performer.

When he gasped that he was ready to pop, Bruno begged for him to do it in his mouth. Sam rammed the swollen tip of his dick into the wet mouth, and soon we saw signs of sperm dribbling from Bruno's mouth.

Now Sam fell to his knees and swallowed Bruno's prick. He used his fists to milk the thick stalk while his mouth sucked loudly on the tip.

"I gotta piss," Bruno cried, "so you'd better get ready for a river of it!" Sam moved back but kept his mouth gaping open. Streams of urine spurted into his mouth and Sam swallowed all of it, as if he had water fountain beneath his fists.

The golden shower was followed by jets of white streaking through the shadows. Sam didn't miss a drop. They took a break and we got fresh beer and drinks. My stepbrother was now the focus of their attention.

"So are you gonna get fucked onstage or not, handsome?" asked Bruno, running his hand over Steve's bicep.

"I've got to see if my butthole can take it," Steve drawled. "I thought maybe, if, well, if I could get a dildo up there, it might be a start."

Bruno jumped up. "A dildo you are gonna get, you hung Hercules from Dixie! Why don't you just bend over the back of this sofa here and let your Uncle Bruno and Sammy fit you up for the perfect dildo."

Sam peeled off his briefs and obeyed and both men rolled their eyes and fanned themselves. Bruno removed a medium-sized dildo shaped like an average erection. He covered it with K-Y and handed the object to Sam.

"You first, Sam."

Sam's cock was rising steadily, though, and as he rubbed Steve's buttocks, he was growing more excited.

"Uh, remember now," Steve said, without looking around, "just the dildo. No real cocks. I'm still not sure."

"Of course, of course," Sam said too quickly. "Just put our hands back on your cheeks, buddy, and spread those beautiful buns."

It was a sight that would have made even the most violent homophobe erect. In the muted lighting, Steve's rippling torso looked even more magnificent in his crouched position. His privates hung down heavily, pressed against the back of the velvet couch.

Sam edged the dildo in carefully, and when Steve didn't protest, he pushed it all the way in.

"How does that feel, Stevie-Roonie?"

"Is it in? I can hardly feel it. Maybe something a little bigger."

Sam glanced at Bruno, who covered his mouth to keep from laughing, and they got an artificial cock found only on a hung stud. This time, Bruno slathered it with lubricant and began to work the dildo in. Steve shifted his feet a little and grunted.

"That feels a little better, but I don't feel too much pressure. Maybe I could take something thicker."

Sam had been stroking his erection until it was at its thickest and most dangerous stage. "Let me try one made with latex. It feels more like a man's cock. Now, it'll be sticky, but—"

Carefully, he pushed his hard-on up into my brother's butt and began fucking him, being careful not to let his hips touch Steve.

"Um, that feels better," Steve grunted, resting his face on his arms. "Warmer and more fleshlike. It—it feels kinda nice."

Sam was silent as he pushed his cock in deeper still careful not to give himself away. I watched in fascination. Could Steve actually believe he was being fucked with a dildo? Was this an act? I was certainly relieved to see him enjoying it, which was astonishing.

He had carried on ever since coming to Manhattan how he would never do this or get sucked. But he sure acted like a man who thoroughly enjoyed a deep screw.

"Let Bruno, try out his latex dildo," Sam whispered, just in time, pulling out and mashing his spurting tip into a wad of paper towel.

Bruno was greatly turned on by Sam's performance and quickly, he began to edge his hard-on up into Steve's sweating white butt.

"This might feel a little different, Steve," Sam called.

"It feels—okay," sighed Steve, still resting his face on his hands, his eyes closed. "I like the latex better. It's not cold, like the first one. You can push it in deeper if you'd like."

Both Bruno and Sam both glanced at me. I just rolled my eyes. I was as startled by Steve's reaction as they were. We had all expected a battle of resistance, but Steve was actually grooving on it all.

Bruno pulled out to shoot out his orgasm into a towel and was replaced by Sam again. Both men impressed me with how quietly they did it.

When Sam ejaculated once more, he wiped his cock clean and slapped Steve's butt playfully. "Okay, partner. You can turn around now. Seems like you handled it pretty well. Whew, you must have! You've got one hell of a hard-on."

Steve smiled and nodded. "All that ass-stuff did get me a little aroused. You—You mind if I unload? I won't mess up anything!"

Bruno whooped. "Honey, you can unload all you want to. It won't be the first time that's happened in here."

I had returned from the bathroom after giving my hand signal just in time to see Steve give a dazzling jerk-off performance. What a superstar he'd be if Matt saw him now. He sat on the back of the cushion, both his fists pulling steadily at his swollen hard-on.

Sam and Bruno watched openmouthed, no doubt wanting to help him out, but content to watch. Steve's testicles shrank steadily until they vanished completely up into his scrotum. His muscles bulged, gleamed with sweat, a lock of his black hair had fallen over his forehead.

Closing his eyes, Steve grunted and arched his hips. Streams of sperm spurted out, spattering both Sam and Bruno, who playfully scooted closer to catch the wetness in their mouths.

For several minutes after that, we all sat still, watching Steve's cock flop up and down, with streams of semen trickling out of the large slit.

"Okay," he laughed, standing up. "Show's over. I guess I won't have any trouble performing Christmas Eve."

The detectives were dejected. They thought surely that either Bruno or Sam would try something on me and my stepbrother.

"Don't you get it?" Ramon tried to explain. "This Bruno and Sam both like the sadistic stuff. They work as a team."

"But I didn't see any of that," I protested. "Bruno didn't even get fisted. Maybe some of his other friends go into all that crap. But all I saw was him and Sam having energetic sex. Nothing more."

"Don't you trust either of them," Butch warned. "Christmas Eve or Christmas Day is when he's striking again. We just know it. You keep that gun handy, you hear me?"

Steve's spirits were buoyed by his experience at

Bruno's, and he seemed to have dropped his suspicions of Sam. His optimism rose even higher when we got home. The Gold Modeling Agency wanted him over instantly. He might be just the man they were looking for in their quest for the Ambrosia Soap Man. If Steve got it, he would be on his way as the handsome hunk who would soap up his body with Ambrosia Soap, sold all over the world.

I was hurrying out of the building on my way to the Ritz when I passed Sam, who had slipped into his security guard uniform.

"Mmm, just thinking of fucking Steve makes me get hard," he grinned. Then he moved closer, his face becoming serious. "Don't slap me when I say this, but your stepbrother is putting on a big act."

"He wants to be an actor, Sam, so—what do you mean?"

"The way his butthole was sucking on my cock means only one thing: he's been getting fucked a lot."

"Of course he did. I told you about his past."

"Fuck his past. No, I mean now, today. I've fucked hundreds of guys and I can tell if they're used to it and like it. Your stepbrother is very used to it, and he loves it. His butt didn't want me to pull out."

"Oh, get off it. He's been a virgin with men since before he joined the Marines."

Sam shrugged and then he said something else that dampened my spirits. "You know he wears a wig? I was down at the Adonis last week, and there was this great-looking hunk with muscles and long, curly hair. And dark glasses. I swear it was Steve, getting blown and fucked in the john."

"Why are you trying to put him down? It wasn't Steve! I swear it. I should know. He's my stepbrother."

"And you saw your stepbrother loving the hell out of being fucked this afternoon. And you'd been telling everybody what a naïve, basically straight guy he is. Sure, sure."

Chapter Nine

The night of the big event was like a glitzy Broadway opening. The street was blocked off. Huge spotlights raked the clear, wintry sky. Any man who was any kind of gay had managed to get a seat.

More than a thousand were turned away. Even

Manhattan's TV stations had sent crews to cover this as part of a "novelty" feature.

Live sex onstage had become chic and daring and colorful. Matt had hired two hot photographers to snap me and Bruno in the throes of sexual fever.

And there was that added bonus of some gorgeous straight boy willing to lose his virginity on stage for $1,000. At Steve's request, his name was never released to the media, but Arthur Bell's *Village Voice* column noted: "He is reportedly a Southern-fried dream who would make even celibates achieve erections. As far as his equipment goes, it's definitely two-handsful, according to those who have seen it. And his rearend? Visualize two bowling balls, painted white, taped together. Get the picture?

I had worked with Steve on his routine but minutes, I saw that his very awkwardness would simply add to his extraordinary attraction.

Now, I wore a sharply tailored business suit of black wool, red tie, white shirt, my hair slicked back. And wire-rimmed glasses. This superconservative look would knock everyone out of their seats when Bruno began stripping it away.

I watched the other performers get the jammed auditorium warmed up. Matt had only the most luscious dreamboats there that night and what dreams they were.

From Washington came Cameron, a sultry, dirty-blond hustler type who looked lean, mean, and available. Naked and slender, he moved slowly down the walkway, tugging hard at his long cock, shaking it at the men grabbing for it and finally giving it our favorite regular, old Petey who gobbled on it while his boyfriend, the unsmiling Lars, pretended not to notice.

Brad from Minnesota had been a star football player who had come out of the closet and made headlines. Now he was twisting his hairy, beefy body to "Macho Man." He finally found his partner in the audience. With legs apart, he stood before a willowy British type who grabbed the former jock's goodies and had Brad squirting in no time.

One seat out front had been reserved and it was only after intermission that I saw my stepbrother take it. Steve wanted to be alone that night—to get prepared to both watch me and Bruno "do it" and then take his turn.

Many eyes focused on him because Steve had never looked more ravishing. We had agreed on a white sweater, the tight khaki pants which looked so good on him, and work boots. A shock of dark hair had fallen over his brow. As if sensing it was me staring at him through the peephole, he stuck up a thumb for approval and grinned.

Then Creedence Clearwater Rival began wailing out "Proud Mary," the lights dimmed, and slowly Bruno and I moved out from opposite sides of the stage.

There was a tremendous whoop and then whistles and wild applause. He and I twisted sensually toward each other, he glowering, rough, powerful, a dark dream lover in his black leather. Me, clean, glowing, a gay Tom Sawyer. One of the gay

125

papers had run a huge ad that morning showing me on one side, bare-chested but grinning at the camera while frowning on the other side was a delicious-looking Bruno.

He grabbed me, pulled me to him, and ripped off my glasses. This was it! Contact at last. My hands ran under his vest to massage the sweaty flesh and down over his leather-covered butt.

We weren't performing now. He pulled off my coat, shirt, tie and tore off his vest and biker's hat. A low bed covered with red leather had been placed in the center of the stage. Somehow we got over there. By now, we were naked and rampant.

Saying nothing, we kissed, sucked at each other's nipples, and then we were sixty-nining. His cock was dark and glossy, like Sam's, and beautifully malleable, bending easily to fit the contours of my mouth.

His mouth felt like warm honey, exhilarating in the way his tongue darted at my slit, the back of the glans. And then he edged it deeper until I felt it squeezing past his tonsils.

Even in that blazing-hot moment, I sensed the powerful spell we had created on the voyeurs. The Supremes were now warning "Stop! In the Name of Love!" another example of Matt's impish choice in music, but hardly anyone stirred out there in the darkness. I was barely aware of my brother's deep-set eyes fixed on us.

Just when I was afraid of ejaculating, Bruno slipped his mouth from my hard-on, brought my legs up around his back and positioned his erection at my rectum.

A special spotlight was beamed on that area now, and since our asses faced the audience, they could plainly see my partner suddenly popping his cock in and working strenuously to bury it in to the hilt.

Now, he began to hump me in deep, slow, powerful thrusts. Someone whistled at the sight. The two photographers were clicking furiously, and I realized then what a practiced sensualist Bruno was. His technique was one that can't be learned overnight. Each lunge made me want to scream with delight.

His sweat dripped down on me, and he mashed his mouth on mine. I looked up. He grinned and winked, as if saying, "We're knocking their socks off, and we're great!"

I noticed his movements speeding up. His breathing became harsher. Then, with a cry, he pulled out, turned over, and held his cock with both hands: streams of sperm shout out into the front row. There was a burst of applause and foot stomping.

But Bruno hadn't forgotten me. He got down on his knees and thrust my hard-on into his mouth and inched it back into his throat. It didn't take long for me to ejaculate into the crowd.

It was over. The theater shook from shouts and whistles and screams of "Bravo! More! More! We Love you!"

Grabbing our clothes, we kissed again and darted from the stage. We were surrounded by the others. Matt pushed through to hug us.

"What a performance! Jesus Christ, watching

you two young pups fuck like that made sex look clean!"

Before we parted, Bruno kissed me again and whispered: "Now, let's do it in private. Tomorrow at my place at three o'clock. Just you and me."

"I'll be there."

I showered quickly, threw on some shorts and a leather vest, and hurried to the side of the stage to watch the next highlight on the program. Matt thrust a bottle of champagne into my hand. We kissed and then watched.

"And now, all you horny young and old men, The Ritz Male Follies is proud to also bring to you on this incredibly fun-filled night, another first. Our next performer is superstraight, from down in Dixie, and he's agreed—for $1,000—to lose his virginity. For just one hour, he'll be gay, like the rest of us. So we now present—Steve!"

There were loud gasps, whistles and ribald shouts of approval as Steve bounded from his seat up to the stage. All of us whooped when the old Billy Ward and the Dominoes rocker, "Sixty-Minute Man," boomed out.

"Get it?" Matt laughed. "For sixty minutes, Steve is gay!"

Even in his clumsy shuffling way, my stepbrother looked incredibly sexy as he grinned sheepishly and kicked off his boots. A blush made him even more adorable, and that made us cheer him on even louder.

His sweater and shirt came off, and now everyone saw what a powerful physique he had. He moved his slacks down slowly, teasing the worshipping crowd until he now stood in just his white skivvies.

Turning his back as I had rehearsed with him, he slowly peeled his B.V.D.s down over his ankles, picked them up and turned, holding the garment over his privates.

He pretended to leave the stage by waving and throwing a kiss; but, as expected, there was an explosion of protest. "Take it off, take it off!"

This time, he threw his undies out into the theater and there were more screams and shouts when they saw the size of his privates. He grabbed his penis at its base and whirled it around, waved, and stood still as the spotlight changed from gold to red.

Quietly, he moved backward until he was at the base of the low bed. He lay back on it, stroking his phallus.

"And now," whispered Eddie over the loudspeaker, "you will see, for the first time, our beautiful young Adonis get fucked by another man. And he'll also get that gourd-sized cock sucked for the first time."

Now Sly and the Family Stone began chanting, "Different strokes for different folks..." Again, I was reminded of how brilliant Matt could be in choosing music to match a mood.

When Bruno came strolling out again, this time nude, I was as startled as everyone else. I had thought it would be one of the other dancers. But the theater exploded with delight. He had captivated everyone with what he had done with me. Now he would do the same with my stepbrother.

129

He settled his body on Steve's and I saw him kiss him. Steve didn't respond at first. He let Bruno do all the work, but then he seemed to forget his rigidity. His arms wrapped around the satyr and his body writhed against his partner's.

Bruno raised his hips so everyone could see that his cock was now hard. Once more, he positioned the gummy tip at Steve's butthole. The special spotlight now showed everything—and there it was, Bruno's swollen dick sliding slowly up into this magnificent straight boy.

We heard him cry out, gasp, and close his eyes. But this time it was he who brought Bruno's face to his. They kissed wildly. Bruno fucked harder and Steve pulled his legs back further to give the dancer more room.

Both gleamed with sweat, and when Bruno finally yanked himself out and blew out his wad for the audience, we could see sweat dripping even from his cock.

In an eerie replay of the earlier scene, Bruno now fell to his knees and crammed Steve's thick erection into his mouth.

Steve seemed to be in a fever. He was panting, gasping, his eyes closed tightly and his hands rubbing his tits. He pushed his hips forward to drive more of his dick down into Bruno's throat.

His mouth was stretched to a grotesque angle, as if he had broken it, but his lips was now pressed against my brother's smooth pubis.

Steve began muttering, "Oh, yeah, I'm 'bout

ready, baby...get ready...pull out now...it's coming up..."

Bruno barely had time to move aside when Steve jumped up, went to the edge of the stage, and used both fists to stroke himself.

As I had seen him do a thousand times, thick, streaks of lubricant jetted out, startling most since it looked as if he were pissing. Then the lines of whiteness sprayed out: pow, pow, powerful gusts.

Steve fell back on the bed, Eddie whispered to everyone, "And there you've just seen our Sixty-Minute Man, Steve, who for a brief time, discovered the joys of gay sex."

The lights dimmed and the theater seemed to explode. Men had jumped to their feet, screamed, whistled, and cried for more.

I had thrown a robe over him and he was surrounded by everyone slapping his shoulder, kissing his cheek.

But he was subdued. "I think I'll just jump into the shower," he said quietly. He vanished into my dressing room.

"Shh," I hissed to the others. "This is a radical moment for him, guys. Let's leave him alone. It'll take some getting used to, you know?"

The others were understanding and hurried around to get ready for their performances.

When Steve appeared, he was dressed in his winter parka and muffler and carried his duffel bag. "I'm worn out," he said, not looking at me. "I need to walk around some. I'm so wound up I can't sleep."

131

"Steve, how do you feel about this?" I said quickly. "I don't want you getting depressed or anything. You feel okay?"

He nodded and walked to the exit. "Yeah, I'm okay. I'll see you later."

I was exhausted when I got home after hours of merrymaking with the others at Matt's lavish suite at the Plaza. Liquor and good food were endless as we celebrated this historic night. Bruno and I said little to each other. We had developed an intense secret bond that needed no words. Our eyes would meet, he would smile slightly in that mysterious way, and I'd nearly come. He was a sensualist's dream, and tomorrow I would enjoy more of it.

Of course, I'd have to alert my detective friends. Their feet were much more on the ground than mine. If I liked someone, I just couldn't see him doing wrong. Steve had taunted me about this trait when we were growing up. I was an old-fashioned Pollyanna. But I'd been taught in church and school that you should look for the best in a person.

When I returned home, I was surprised to find Steve asleep. He was curled up in a ball, his back to me, a sure sign that he wanted no touchy-feelie tonight.

But I refused to let his moodiness bother me. It was he who was so insistent on going through with the whole thing. He wanted the thousand, and so he had gotten fucked and sucked in public. That would always be there in his past until he died.

I awoke once that night. Steve wasn't there in bed. He was standing at the window, naked, staring out at the darkness. The expression on his face was one of desperation.

CHAPTER TEN

I hurried along the icy sidewalks, past shards of frozen snow, beneath a curtain of sleet.

Since last night, the world had changed. From a clear, crystal night, it had turned into a grim winter scene. The only thing that persuaded me to get out on such a god-awful afternoon was my lusty thoughts of seeing Bruno again.

I had hesitated in even telling my detectives. Ramon was thrilled. "This could be it! If he is the killer, then we'll know for sure."

Then Butch had gotten on the phone: "Don't you leave your apartment unless you tell us, and then we'll follow you. We promise. For God's sake, take your gun and go to the bathroom window as soon as you get there. Put some kind of bottle out there. If you don't, we'll bust in. And don't set foot in his building unless you see an old green van parked nearby. It'll have a rag tied to the antenna. That's us. You got it, baby?"

I felt the old Bud beer bottle in my jacket pocket. And touched the cold metal of the gun in my other. Even in this weather, I sensed strongly I was being followed.

On the subway, I had time to flash back over the night before and that morning. Most of my fans must have imagined me luxuriating beneath silk sheets, my body entwined with either Bruno or some other glorious-looking hunk. What I had done, after swallowing some Alka-Seltzer for my head and a pot of hot coffee was to prepare for a frenetic day.

Steve and I were to be completely out of our apartment in just four days. I began throwing things into boxes, starting with mine first. There was a constant barrage of phone calls from the other dancers, from Matt, from reporters and gay columnists. It was Christmas Day! Surely I could drop by for a few minutes to drink some champagne, meet some of my fans, have some hot fun!

After all, I was off that night, and we weren't expecting a big crowd. Most were at home, or with families, or had hurried out of town after seeing the Ritz spectacular.

Steve had left me a note saying he had an early-morning appointment at his modeling agency. He was among the finalists for the Ambrosia Soap Man commercial. "Sorry for my mood last night. When I get home, you'll see I've changed." I was surprised that Steve would be called for an audition on Christmas Day. After seeing Bruno, I planned to prepare an old-fashioned holiday feast for just my stepbrother and me. We had no other relatives, we were together, alone in the biggest city in the world.

This would be a special night for us both. And perhaps, later, I would discover how much he had really changed.

Before I left my studio, I went to Sam O'Brien's room. Surely he wouldn't be there on Christmas Day! He had so many sex partners that I could see him servicing them all, even if it was a day to stay home.

To my surprise, he answered his door quickly. As usual, he wore nothing, but his eyes were red and his face was pasty. "Oh, me head, me head!" he groaned, staring at me through scrunched up eyes. "May I live and breathe, if it's not the blond bombshell! Why aren't you on stage, getting fucked by my favorite fucker!"

"Merry Christmas, Sammy!" I laughed. He always had a way of cheering me up by being so impudent. "Are you going to be in tonight? I'm fix-

137

ing a big old-fashioned feast for me and Steve. Wanna come by for a drink afterward?"

He pulled at his cock, which hung heavy and dark down his thighs. He startled me by grabbing my shoulders and shaking me. "Look, be very careful today, my golden-haired slut. You don't seem to realize how dangerous things are. With everybody gone, this would be a perfect time for the killer to strike!"

I pulled away and kissed his cheek. "Cut it out, Sam. I know what I'm doing. Now, I've got to go meet someone."

"You aren't going to Bruno's? Don't lie—I know you are. Listen, I wouldn't go there."

"You certainly seem to enjoy visiting him for hot sex."

"That's different."

He ran a hand over his face and pulled me close against him again. Once more, I realized what a powerful man he was, how much bigger he was than me. "I have a feeling things are moving together very fast. If you need me for anything, come straight to me, in this room. You understand? You'll be safe here."

He let me go and stared down at me. He was acting so strange. When he turned to pick up a bottle of liquor, I understood. "Sam, you've got to stop hitting the bottle so much. It's only noon."

He grinned like his old self again and flapped his cock at me. "I sure hope we'll get together for some fun tonight. That's your Christmas present to me."

"And yours to me! But after a visit with Bruno, I don't know if I'll have any energy left."

"Remember what I said," he whispered and shut the door.

Past liquor stores with blinking Christmas lights, past thrift shops with ratty-looking Santa Claus masks in the windows, past little hole-in-the-wall newsstands where the dark-faced owners stood shivering, staring at me glumly, with small piles of snow collecting on their stacks of unsold newspapers and magazines.

The side street looked desolate—gray, black and white. Not even the usual winos and homeless were out today. Bruno's warehouse building resembled a funeral home. Before stepping in, though, I looked around. Then I saw the van parked up ahead. From a radio aerial, a rag fluttered in the wind. I pulled the fur collar of my new trench coat up higher and rang the buzzer.

"Come up," the voice said. The door clicked open. The freight elevator was freezing; a ripped bag of potato chips crunched on the floor, a dead mouse in the corner. I shivered, but not only from the cold.

My excitement about getting back together with Bruno was fast ebbing. Now, all I really wanted to do was to be home in a hot bath, sipping some champagne, then going to bed for a much-needed nap and then fixing supper my stepbrother and me.

The doors opened. Chic was belting out "Good Times" and the warmth felt wonderful. I forgot my misgivings.

"Say, Brunny," I called out, using my nickname

for him. "Show me your ass and make it quick. I'm freezing!"

"Back here!" a voice called out. Instantly, the chill returned but not from winter. The voice on the intercom, and now from here—*it wasn't Bruno's!*

"Bruno! Where are you?" I called out again, looking around me. Chic had finished their number, and now The Supremes were wailing, "Stop! In the Name of Love!"

I wrapped my fingers around the gun handle and pulled it from my coat pocket. Bruno loved to joke, to kid, but he wouldn't turn our rendezvous into a joke. Like me, he had felt something powerful flow between us onstage, more than just sex.

I moved quietly past the orgy room. The door was open and as I moved closer I saw those life-sized mannequins and blow-up dolls hanging from the ceiling.

Somewhere a door closed softly.

I whirled around, but saw nothing. Something was wrong here. I felt somebody else near. Very near! I looked up then and fell back.

Hanging down between two male mannequins was Bruno's nude body. A black leather rope had snapped his neck. His beautiful body had been sliced to shreds. A long slit in his stomach. Entrails hung glistening. And below, the center of his young universe—

Next to him hung what resembled a toy lion. Only the ragged hole where its head had once been suggested it had once been alive. Bruno's beloved little Lambchop!

I didn't have time to stand there, though. I heard shouts of: "Brett! It's the police!" And suddenly I was in the arms of Butch and Ramon while a half dozen more officers swarmed into the room.

Then, like me, they froze, staring up at those dead eyes staring down at us.

CHAPTER ELEVEN

My detectives took me to the emergency room of
St. Vincent's Hospital for some medication to calm
me down.

They questioned me for hours about Bruno and
possible suspects. We all knew he lived a life-style
that would have been considered bizarre by many.

But, as my former stage lover said to me several times, "I've never hurt anybody. When I get into some wild scenes with my partner, we both know exactly what we're getting into. We respect each other's boundaries. When they say, 'Enough,' I stop. And vice versa."

"That was a warning of some kind," Butch told me grimly. "Someone's trying to warn you, Brett, to watch out. Somehow this guy is involved with you and with Bruno."

They wanted me out of the Vanderbilt Arms by that night. Someone was watching me closely, they said, and I was to go nowhere—not even to the Ritz—without letting them know ahead of time.

"But what about Steve? I can't leave him alone. We were getting together tonight."

"Fuck your stepbrother now!" Butch snapped. "It's you who's in danger—not your damned stepbrother. He's grown. We'll tell him what we've done."

His face softened when he added, "He'll appreciate what we're trying to do. If we ever get this sleazy wacko, it'll be in the next few days."

A police car would patrol my area every few minutes until I moved out. In the meantime, I was to get the few things I needed and then go to the lobby.

The security guards in my lobby were warned to be on special alert and let no one in who did not live there. The two Puerto Ricans regarded me with awe as I went to the elevator. I must be very special to create this concern.

Steve still had not come home. I stripped and

threw on a robe. I had to shower away that whole obscene afternoon, put on something fresh and clean. I couldn't see myself even wearing my expensive new trench coat again. It would always remind me of having worn it to Bruno's murder scene. I hurried around the apartment, throwing things into my bag.

I needed another bag for my toiletries and saw the duffel bag Steve always carried with him each day. He wouldn't mind if I used it now.

Opening it, I smiled when I saw a neatly folded pair of white Jockey shorts and jockstrap. They were so like Steve that I pressed them against my face. I could sniff a bit of his spermy, macho scent. Some bottles of vitamins, toothpaste, toothbrush, small bars of hotel soap still wrapped, a travel-sized bottle of Old Spice cologne.

A tuft of dark hair protruded from the bottom. I lifted the flap and stared, my heart suddenly beating so hard I felt dizzy.

A whole secret world lay in that small partition: a long, curly wig, a shorter one, of blond curls— and lying across all this was a slab of deadly metal: an old-fashioned straight razor.

Somehow I stood up, backed away, holding the bag in my hand. Then somehow I was knocking on Sam's door.

"Sam! Hurry, let me in!"

He opened it quickly, still naked. "What? What?"

Inside his room, he closed the door. I held up the bag. "Sam, I can't believe it! It can't be my own stepbrother!"

145

"Holy shit!" he muttered, his gaze transfixed by the grotesque objects. "Wigs! A razor. Sit down on the bed, baby, let me give you a drink."

"Sam, I can't turn my own stepbrother in! Steve can explain it all."

The Irishman gave me a glass of brandy and I gulped it down, shivering as its fiery path made its way into my stomach. He sat down beside me on the bed, pulled me close, and kissed my face.

"Don't worry and don't say anything to the cops. You don't want to see your stepbrother locked up on circumstantial evidence."

The liquor was working at an incredible speed. My face glowed. I let Sam take the bag and put it on his desk. He joined me again and began kissing me.

"I know I've been hard on your stepbrother," he whispered, rubbing his penis against my hand. "I was only playing with you. I knew how much you loved him and not me. I wanted you to love me, but saw that it was Bruno and that I'd never win."

He had forced me to lie back on his bed. The room swam more rapidly. What had he put in my drink? Liquor didn't act this fast!

He had moved his strong body over mine now. His warm lips made me shiver even as I struggled to sit up. "Sam, please don't! Not now. We've got to think. Steve's in trouble..."

I was finding it difficult to talk, though, and felt Sam opening my robe and kissing my nipples. I tried to push him away, furious for once that his obsession for sex was taking precedence over my crisis.

"Sam, goddamn you, stop it! This is critical! My stepbrother Steve—"

I felt him enter me and, with a grunt of delight, he began to fuck me, seeming to enjoy my struggle to escape. In my woozy state, I watched him pause for a moment and reach over the side of the bed.

He clamped a ratty-looking wig on his head. "Surprise?" he grinned. "You've seen this before?"

"Sam! No—not you? But it can't be! I found all that stuff in Steve's bag!"

He rolled his eyes and stuck out his tongue. "Ever hear of actors using makeup for their auditions? That's all it is. He told me. Wanted to surprise you. And the razor? Steve's got a tough beard. He uses the razor before an audition. Nothing else."

I managed to bring my knee up against his nuts. He gasped, I rolled over and fell to the floor. Desperately, I struggled to get up and move to the door.

He locked it and I turned to look up as he snapped a long length of black leather coil between his hands.

"Slut! You tempted me from the very beginning more than anyone else! And I knew that each time I did it, I was committing sin—and you were the reason!"

He dragged me back to bed, but the liquor was wearing off, and my energy flooded back. I threw my fist so hard in his face that he fell back. I dove for the door again. He threw me back on the

147

bed, grinning savagely, as if enjoying our struggle.

He crammed his hard-on up into me again. I tried to bite his nipples, his chest—but he slapped me hard. This time his face was contorted into a terrifying mask.

"Slut! Slut! You should have been destroyed long ago, but I used all the others as substitutes and—"

I was certain I was drunk when suddenly the door burst open—and in rushed my detective buddies, another mob of policemen—and my stepbrother.

"Get your cock out of him, O'Brien!" Ramon shouted, grabbing Sam's wig and staring at it in a moment of hilarious perplexity.

"What the shit—a wig, Goddammit!"

But Sam had gotten to his feet now and looked the same as ever—grinning impishly and stroking his cock. Without any warning, he ejaculated, spattering the pants legs of both Ramon and Butch.

"Goddamn you!" Butch screeched. "Messing up my britches!"

Steve had come over to me and helped me to my feet. I pulled my robe together and hugged him.

"We thought it was O'Brien all along," Butch said. "Your stepbrother helped us. He's been with us all day because we knew if we gave this creep the chance, he'd finally fuck up."

"That was a great fuck, blondie," Sam smiled as he pulled on his pants. "When I get out, we'll have more."

"You're never getting out, you fucking sleaze-ball," shouted Ramon. "You and that fucking priesthood. God help the Catholic church when it keeps shitting out crap like you."

Steve and I spent Christmas afternoon giving our depositions.

I still found it impossible to believe—my handsome, oversexed neighbor down the hall had actually butchered all those men—and had wanted to add me to his list.

Butch took me and Steve to a corner diner. Over steaming mugs of black coffee and bowls of chili and crackers, he gave us a rundown on what had happened.

"We knew that if Sam O'Brien thought you were being taken away and he'd never see you again, then he would have to strike."

"You mean you knew what he planned to do to me?" I gasped, not only from the idea but from the fiery hot chili. I gulped down a glass of water.

"We had to. You trust everybody you like, Brett." He smiled. "Nothing we said would have changed your mind about Sam O'Brien."

"But someone was at Bruno's loft! How could Sam have done it and still be at home when I got there?"

"In his insane world, he wanted to both scare you away, to make you never see him again and then he wanted to taunt you. He was incredibly jealous of you and Bruno."

"Detective," Steve broke in, "please let me and my stepbrother just go home. It's Christmas, you know, and—"

"Of course." Butch laughed. Before parting, we shook hands. "You still be careful, Brett. New York's a jungle. There are still animals out there."

A police cruiser took us home, but the driver permitted me to dash into Sam's Gourmet on Broadway to pick up some goodies for supper.

Back in the apartment, Steve put the grocery bags down and turned to me. Saying nothing, we embraced and kissed for a long time.

"I—" he began.

I put my hand over his lips. "Wait. Before we say anything, let's clean up, put on our robes, and we'll have champagne and turkey. Then we'll talk."

In the shower, we soaped each other up, laughing as we tried to tickle each other. I grabbed Steve's cock, stretched it out, and pretended to scrub it. It puffed up quickly, but I released it, not wanting to do anything until we got in bed. For I was certain that this night would finally give me my stepbrother as a lover.

Wearing a new oversized robe of white terry-cloth, I lit candles and Steve came out of the shower, drying his hair. He wore nothing and looked scrumptious.

Pouring champagne into the goblets, I gave him his and we toasted each other.

"May things have finally changed for the best," I said.

"May tonight be one we'll never forget." He smiled and winked.

I had spread out our gourmet goodies on the table: a huge turkey, mounds of dressing, stuffed mushrooms, baked beans, piles of steaming rolls, glowing with butter. And on the counter were apple, sweet potato and chess pies and for Steve, his favorite: a huge coconut cake.

"Well, stepbrother of mine," I began, "let's talk. You were so sure of Sam O'Brien. Why?"

Steve stood against the windows, still nude, and stared into his champagne. "We all make mistakes. So you looked into my duffel bag."

He lifted his gaze to stare accusingly at me.

"Yes, I did because I needed one for—Steve, what were those wigs and that razor for? Sam said you used them for auditions and—"

"I'll show you."

He opened the bag and shook out the wig. Putting it on his head, it completely transformed him. "All actors need props."

Next he removed the razor. With a flick, it flew open—glinting in the candlelight. I put my champagne down uneasily.

"Steve—why the razor? Sam said you needed to shave close before an audition, but there are other razors, smaller ones."

He moved toward me, smiling strangely, and eased my discomfort by closing the sheath of metal and placing it back in the bag. But then he brought up a mass of darkness. I watched him let it drop to the floor—as if it were a long snake.

"Steve, what is it? A leather coil? A rope?"

He reached into his bag again and brought out dark glasses which he placed over his eyes. I got up from my chair and moved away. There was something terrible going on here.

You were always tempting me, little brother, to be like you, like Stepdaddy. You know what Stepdaddy did to me! He ruined me and then I knew I wanted to be like him, too."

I edged around the table. The door was behind him. If I could just get past him—

"Steve, what's wrong? It's been a horrible day for us both. You don't know how grateful I am for helping the cops capture Sam."

"He's nuts!" Steve shouted, his face hardening even more and his eyes glaring at me. "I don't what his game is, but he didn't do any killing! Each time I offed one of those stripper sluts, I pretended it was you. I didn't want to kill you so I did one of them and I thought it'd help because you were always after my body, my dick, and if I gave it to you I'd be just like Stepdaddy."

"Steve, please, let's sit down and talk quietly. Put down the rope, get away from your bag—"

He snapped the rope again closer to my face. "I was there in Bruno's place when you came by. I was going to do you like I did him, for fucking me onstage. I was coming at you when I thought—no, no, it's my stepbrother."

I had a knife hidden on the windowsill, behind the curtain. One of those innumerable weapons I had hidden earlier. Now, I edged toward it.

"You murdered Bruno? Steve, why? He thought he was bringing you joy!"

"He destroyed me again, just like Stepdaddy did! The sin never dies, and I liked what he did to me! I liked it!"

He lowered his head, his mouth became small

and thin, like the way I saw it as a child when he would rage against Stepdaddy.

"You let that oil flow into the stove the morning Stepdaddy lit it, didn't you Steve? You killed him."

"I sure did," he said simply, like a little boy boasting. "He deserved it. He used his big dick like a sword that destroyed me."

"You aren't destroyed," I said eagerly. "Come on and let's get dressed. We can catch a plane for someplace down south and get away from everything."

I lunged for the knife, but Steve was faster. He leaped toward me and threw the cord around my throat.

"I didn't want to do this, little brother, but we don't deserve to live."

Before I blacked out, I remember seeing a replay of an earlier scene. My apartment door flew open suddenly, and in rushed my detective buddies again, a small army of cops—and Sam O'Brien.

Outside the wind was freezing and strong, blowing scraps of old newspapers against us.

Steve sat unmoving in the back of the police car. A strange grin flitted across his lips, and when he glanced at me, he winked.

Sam had his arm around me, keeping the mob of reporters and thrill seekers at bay. He had actually been an undercover detective with the NYPD, one of the first openly gay officers hired. From the beginning, he and the others suspected that I was somehow the main object of the killer's desire since I was the most famous gay blond stripper in Manhattan.

And they were certain that the murderer was a person who was close to me. When they discovered that the slayings had begun only after Steve moved to Manhattan, they zeroed in on him.

Sam, wearing a heavy coat and boots and hat, looked down at me, kissing my cheek. "I'm really sorry we had to put you through all this shit, kid. We knew Steve was going to off you anytime because he had finally accepted he was gay on that stage that night. And, tragically, he'd been so brainwashed into thinking it was evil that he would do something dramatic."

They theorized that the only way to make Steve finally make his strike at me was for him to drop his facade since Sam had been arrested.

"They were outside listening," Sam continued, "so I had to make it sound fucking convincing, like I really was the psycho. That must have tickled your stepbrother a hell of a lot. I just couldn't resist splashing my come on my detective buddies. Ha, they're gonna pay me back!"

"It hasn't hit me yet," I murmured, watching the car taking my stepbrother drive away and some of the TV vans giving chase. Suddenly another van screeched to a stop beside us and a man with curly hair, whom I recognized as one of the reporters, stuck his head out the window.

"You hear about the new gay murder?" he shouted. "We just got it on the police monitor! Found the body just a block away. Another gay stripper. Same size as the others. Blond hair. Worked at the

Ramrod. They think it happened just in the last hour or two—"

My eyes met Sam's. "Oh, God! That means—"

He closed his eyes tight and slammed his fist against the police car. "Don't say it—don't say it! There's another serial killer on the loose!"

The wind whistled around us, hurtling biting snow against our faces. Old leaves suddenly whirled around on the sidewalks, like skeletons dancing together.

"I thought it was over, Sam," I whispered.

He hugged me to him as we walked back to my building. "No, it's only the beginning."

Dark snow clouds skimmed and curled above, heralding another storm.

"I run to Death and Death meets me as fast and all my pleasures are like yesterday."